These stories are unsettling in
they get under your skin and take root.
horror, and all the uncanny spaces in bet
in small moments and everyday objects, with characters that are
so well observed we feel like we already know them. Beautifully
written, delightfully queer, and always unexpected.
Rachel Plummer
Wain

*

In Ryan Vance's writing, new dimensions of possibility
meet the depths of human nature. A freakish, festering
and occasionally beautiful collection of stories.
Laura Waddell
Exit

*

Vance's fantasy elements are all the more enchanting
for being so close to reality. The mix of magic and the everyday
will linger with readers long after the book is shut.
Publisher's Weekly

*

Ryan Vance's collection *One Man's Trash* is a welcome addition
to the genre, not just creating his own myths and legends,
but adapting and updating classics.
Gutter Magazine

*

So very queer and fantastical, the stories of *One Man's Trash*
(nothing rubbish here!) push the reader one step closer to the weird.
Matthew Bright
Stories to Sing in the Dark

Published by Lethe Press
lethepressbooks.com

'Babydog' first appeared in *Mycelia #1* (2018) / 'Mischief' first appeared as 'The Pit King' in *F[r]iction #10* (2018) / 'Mouthfeel' first appeared in *Gutter Magazine #16* (2017) / 'The Cowry House' first appeared in *Dark Mountain #9* (2016) / 'The Offset and The Calving' first appeared in *Gutter Magazine #15* (2016) / 'Finch and Crow do the Alleycat' first appeared in *New Writing Scotland #34* (2016) / 'Love in the Age of Operator Errors' first appeared as 'Contamination' in *The Grind Journal* (2016) / 'Other Landscapes are Possible' first appeared as 'Ten Love Songs' in *The Grind Journal* (2016) / 'Gold Star' first appeared in *Out There: An Anthology of LGBT Writing* (2014)

'One Man's Trash', 'Asterion', 'When All We've Lost is Found Again', 'The Naples Solider', 'Dead Skin', 'The Ballygilbert Gasser', and 'Other Landscapes Are Possible' are all original to this collection.

Cover Design by Ryan Vance
Interior design by Ryan Vance

ONE MAN'S TRASH

STORIES

BY
RYAN VANCE

For the magpies.

CONTENTS

ONE MAN'S TRASH

A damaged hand, turned palm up and empty, as if offering something invisible. Red welts on the undersides of the knuckles, blue waterproof plasters on the fingers. Otto studied it closely, expecting to find some small piece of useless tat nestled in the palm. He looked then at the face of the man offering him nothing. Sharp cheekbones, afro hair styled into a flat-top. Young and handsome, underfed. Most men grimaced when under Otto's influence, with pain or anticipation or even relief, as if Otto had freed some giving urge long untended within them.

This man wore an expression which Otto couldn't parse.

'Three twenty,' the man repeated. 'Please.'

Cups clattered, steam screeched. Reality crashed into Otto like a shower of stones. This was a cafe, a place of commerce.

'I don't have any money,' he said. Between them on the counter sat Otto's latte, steaming in its paper cup. Not for years had anything felt quite so unattainable. 'Can't I just take it?'

'Fuck sake, I'll pay for it,' said a woman behind him. She dumped a rattle of change into the barista's outstretched hand and walked out the door with Otto's coffee.

He held on to the hope that his usual charm had merely been delayed. Any moment now, an expression of agonised anticipation was about to bloom across the barista's face and, like the other men, he would try and force something into Otto's hands. Another coffee, or something closer to hand: a clutch of napkins, the paper money from the till.

Instead, the barista looked like he should've been anywhere but here, his gaze flat but active, alternating between Otto and the clock which hung above the till. Otto realised he was expected to leave empty-handed. Outside, decaffeinated and chilly under a winter sun, Otto gripped the push-bar of his driftwood cart. He tried to understand what had gone wrong. He'd called ahead to place his order, so it could be waiting for him when he arrived, his name already written on the cup, to avoid any hassle. But today's barista was a new hire, and their newness had bucked Otto's routine. First, their refusal to take orders over the phone. Then, on arrival, Otto had to choose something from the chalkboard, which should have been a red flag. Finally, the ritual of payment, which in Otto's experience happened only to other people.

He pushed his cart past other shops and restaurants and wondered if they would also deny him service. It depended, of course, on who stood behind the till. A man? Otto's ability would force them to give him something, anything at all. A woman? He might as well go begging. As far as Otto could discern, gender was the sole limit to this strange and passive spell. This new barista up-ended that theory.

Up ahead a homeless man sat bundled against the side of a rubbish bin. Under ordinary circumstances, Otto often chose to spare the desperately needy, but not today. He wanted to test himself, he wanted to test his gift. As Otto drew closer, a glazed expression stole over the rough sleeper's bearded face, and he thrashed out of his sleeping bag, to present it draped over both arms like a stretch of fine silk. *So far, so good*, thought Otto, but he needed to be certain.

He strung out the act until the man dropped to his knees, on the verge of tears, begging him to please for gods sake take the bag take the bag please please *take the fucking bag*.

'No,' said Otto.

The man screamed and dashed his face against the side of the driftwood cart, which was reassuring.

'Oh, for heaven's sake,' said Otto. 'Give it here.'

The bag went in the cart, and Otto left the man shivering in the cool sunlight, blood dripping from his nose. The next man to pass Otto forced into his arms a leather suitcase full of papers. The third, a single shoe, which Otto later threw off a bridge into a river. He couldn't sell a single shoe. After ten minutes of trundling and gifting, he made it home.

A woman stood in the doorway to his building, arms folded, blonde hair a-frizz, dumpy body hidden inside a man's pinstripe suit. 'Where the fuck you been?' she said.

'I didn't go far, Sheila.'

She hated that he called her Sheila, never *mum* or *ma* or *mammy*. The second he'd learnt how to use a microwave, Sheila had stopped being his mother. The way Otto saw it, there was nothing she could give him which he couldn't get from any passing Tom, Dick or Harry.

'What if something happened to you?' she asked, already rummaging through the cart. 'How would I get by? You shouldn't go out alone.' She held a plain silver tie pin up to the light. 'Been ages since we had any good sparkles. What happened to that nice young fella with all the jewellery? Give him a ring.' She laughed at her own joke.

Otto remembered exactly what had happened. He'd found the 'nice young fella' through a dating app and yes, he'd been quite the peacock, dripping with 'sparkles' in every photo. Their first meeting in real life took place on Otto's doorstep, and off came the emerald brooch. Drinking wine on the sofa, three opal ear studs. By the time Otto kicked him out of bed, the man had parted with his clothes, seven rings, a gold chain, his wallet and three fair-to-middling orgasms. With nothing more to gift and a wild unhappy look in his eyes, the man had walked naked, shell-shocked, into the dawn light, and threw himself straight under the first train to leave the station. The only thing he hadn't given away was his name.

Foolish, really, for Otto to have taken the poor peacock to bed. There were limits to how much of themselves men could offer someone like him.

'I'm just saying,' Sheila continued, 'a ruby here, a diamond there, it does help pay the bills.' She lifted a bundle of jumpers and shirts out of the cart and trudged upstairs to the spare bedroom, where she'd organised a small photography studio, and would spend the morning taking pictures to spread around various bidding websites.

When Otto was nine, she'd promised their oft-absent landlord a clandestine agreement, a ruse to bring the crooked oaf within range of Otto's power. She'd handcuffed the man to a radiator, sat Otto on his lap, and by midnight he'd gifted the house to them in perpetuity. This meant rent was no longer a worry, though bills and council tax were still an annoyance. So whatever Otto brought in that they did not want for themselves, they sold online. It kept them comfortable, but not *too* comfortable. Such was life.

Otto, who had done his bit for the day, went for a hot bath to clear his head. Lying back in the tub, however, he couldn't help but see above him in the swirls of steam the barista's scowling face. He felt owed. It disturbed him.

He waited until Sheila had refilled the cart with packages destined for buyers, then asked to chaperone her to the Post Office—more of a statement than a question. 'It'll be hassle,' she warned, and so it was. Even before they reached the end of their street, a man insisted Otto take his wedding ring. Sheila had to scare off the wife, who was less than impressed with the transaction. Sheila bit at the air and pulled her own hair and growled, after which the wife shrewdly turned her anger on her husband, and Otto walked off with the ring adorning his own finger. At the Post Office, Sheila chained the cart to a lamppost and instructed Otto to wait outside, hidden down a cobbled back alley, to avoid further chaos.

Not a chance. Otto slunk back to the cafe, determined to get to the bottom of his morning embarassment. The afternoon clientele were mostly young mothers with children, fresh off the school run. The same barista stood behind the machine, twisting knobs and pushing buttons. He recognised Otto. 'Flat white, yeah?'

'Thank you...' Otto spared a quick glance at the barista's name tag, bright green against the white uniform. '...Toshin?'

'That's not how you say it,' Toshin sighed. 'Take-away?'

'I think I'll sit in.'

Toshin brought the coffee to Otto's table without a flicker of philanthropy. Otto's stomach flipped. He'd have a bill to settle, for sure, and had brought nothing but empty pockets. Would a stranger's wedding ring for a coffee be too generous a trade?

There was one other man present, a father nursing a pot of tea. His two little boys had spread jam on their toast, on their hands, on the table. The father was trying to clean up the mess but his hands shivered hard enough to shake the sticky napkins to the floor. He kept looking over at Otto, his jaw clenched tight in fury or concentration. 'I want to pay,' he growled. He clicked his fingers at the barista. 'I want to pay!' He slapped his sticky table with open palms, causing everyone present to jump and fall silent. The older of his two boys began to cry. 'What's the bill? What do I owe? Tell me!'

Toshin stammered out an answer. The man dug coins from his trouser pocket, more than needed, and flung them across the room. They clattered off the coffee machine and rattled under the fridge. He seemed to skid across the floor to slam his cup and saucer down on Otto's table.

'There!' he shouted. He shoved the plate at Otto once, twice, spilling tea. 'It's mine now, isn't it? So take it! Take the fucking thing!'

Otto gave a nod so slight it was noticed by only the man, who stopped shaking. 'I see you,' the man hissed. 'Every day. Creeping up and down this street, doing whatever the hell this is. Fucking no-good thief.'

The man grabbed his children by the wrists and pulled them out of the cafe without looking back. Toshin counted the scattered change, then stood over Otto. He tipped the contents of Otto's mug into a paper cup with a steady hand, and refused to make eye contact. 'Get out.'

Otto tensed. 'Don't I deserve an apology? That man was very rude.'

'He settled your bill,' said Toshin. 'And then some.'

Otto wondered what would happen if he refused the drink. Would Toshin turn suicidal like the others, when refused? Would he take a cake slice to his chest? Boil his head in the coffee machine's steam jet? Or was he exempt from that madness, too?

Something unfamiliar in Otto didn't want to put Toshin to the test, so he accepted the takeaway cup and left.

En route to the Post Office, Otto was given half a dozen strangers' coats, which he slung over his free arm in a pile, not caring if any slipped to the pavement, and was also gifted a dildo shaped like a dolphin. What some folk carried on their person never failed to surprise him. He dropped the whole lot into the empty cart with a thud.

'Careful, love,' said Sheila, exiting the Post Office. 'I know a fella who'd pay very handsome for that wee electric delight. See you got your coffee, too.'

'Yes,' said Otto. He poured it into a gutter, bitter, and threw the paper cup into a hedge.

On their way home Sheila tried engaging him in conversation about changes in postage pricing, but he was too stewed in his thoughts of Toshin to listen. His mind fizzed like old silver in cola, thick tarnish lifting to reveal a shine he'd tried to forget. A man who could give him nothing, a man he owed nothing to?

That was a man he could treasure.

In the following days, Otto enlisted Sheila to carry small gifts for him to the cafe: a fedora, a belt, a USB stick, a satchel, some half-empty bottles of aftershave, a potted plant with a little life left, a leather-bound journal with a few pages written in a spidery hand. Toshin left the gifts sitting next to the till untouched, but they were always gone by morning. Otto would go rooting through the cafe's bins by moonlight, and find no trace of the trinkets. Proof of acceptance, as far as Otto was concerned.

But where was the reciprocal warmth Otto knew he was due? He ordered glasses of tap water with a slice of lemon, for he feared what might ensue should he have a bill to pay. Toshin's requests to be left alone went unheeded. He felt there must be something specific Toshin wanted, something that would unlock his affection.

So the gifts became more lavish: sparkles, laptops, a remote control drone, a collection of rare stamps, a vintage bike. He presented each with a song, a dance, a flood of words stating the obvious, that something magical connected the two of them, or rather, something not magical at all. Toshin was a garbage chute that gobbled up Otto's incorrigible propensity for consumption and recycled it into charity. A sure sign they should be together, an old-fashioned love, why couldn't Toshin see the truth of it? Otto began to follow Toshin after he finished his shifts at the cafe, a string of rejected and broken men trailing them to the subway, where Otto gave up only because he wasn't allowed to take his cart on the train.

One night, a few months into the courtship, Sheila barged in on him while he was taking a bath. 'What the fuck you playing at?' she screamed. 'Giving our expensive shit to that pretty man of yours! Can't fucking pay the bills with second-hand underpants, can I?' She proceeded to throw bars of soap at his head.

He sloshed about in the water, his bare skin squeaking up the side of the enamel. 'Think I'm content cooped up with you?' Otto screamed back. 'Living off leftovers?'

Sheila laughed at him, then—laughed and laughed and laughed, out into the corridor where she laughed some more.

'There's special websites for underpants!' Otto shouted after her. 'They pay extra for skidmarks!'

He listened to her crash out into the street. From the bathroom window he watched her begin loading heavy items into his cart. Too rattled to dress, thinking only to wrap a towel around his waist, he darted outside half naked, steaming in the night air. Neighbours peeked out their windows but didn't dare intervene.

'That's my cart,' he said.

'The fuck it is, pal.'

Sheila dumped a coil of ethernet cable into the cart. The yellow line zipping out of sight caused Otto's heart to thud in his chest. His cart, he realised, had become her cart. It was piled high with electrical goods, warm clothing, a pair of sleeping bags—all the basics needed to turn a squat into a home. They'd done it once before. She planned to do it again. But this time, without him.

He threw himself in front of the cart. 'I don't know what you do for me,' he said.

'It's called work, pet.' Sheila shoved him out of the way. 'Give it a go some day, you might like it!'

'No, really,' Otto whined. 'I don't know any passwords, or accounts, or anything. I just bring the stuff home.'

Sheila stuck her hands in her hair, ready to pull and scream, but he'd seen that act too many times to be scared by it. He rolled his next words around in his mouth, testing them for potency.

'Stay, please... *Mummy*?'

Sheila relaxed and smiled. At last, he thought, he'd given her what she wanted, and in return he'd got what he wanted. The perfect exchange.

Otto made to grab the push-bar, but her smile had been a prelude, an emotionless showing of teeth. In one motion Sheila hooked a thumb inside his mouth, yanked him down to her level and bit into his bare shoulder.

He beat at her face but she sank her teeth deeper until he could feel the enamel slicing into muscle. The pain brought him to his knees, and her down with him, her hand still in his mouth, as if she wanted to push the awful words back into him by force.

With some effort Sheila relaxed her bite, wiped blood from her mouth and sighed.

'The worst of it is,' she said, 'you'll barely notice I'm gone.'

With a mighty shove she rolled the cart over both his legs and rumbled off into the night.

He snapped back to consciousness once to find a dog licking at his bloodied shoulder, a second time to the sound of his home being ransacked, and a third as the rising sun shone down on his bruised and naked form, his towel missing. Several strangers had placed in its stead a skipping rope, a neat stack of pound coins and a half-drunk bottle of beer.

Some time between dawn and the morning rush hour, he must have pulled his throbbing, broken body along the dirty ground to flop, exhausted, at the door to Toshin's cafe. He couldn't remember the journey, but he remembered the motive. Here came Toshin now, out of uniform but keys in hand. He caught sight of Otto, swore, turned away—and then turned back.

And Otto knew he'd won.

The barista reached out a hand, pulled Otto up into an awkward clasp and led him to a booth indoors. He promised not to call the emergency services. Otto nodded. He respected how even in a crisis, this man refused to give too much away to someone so down on their luck. There was a cold honesty to it which felt familiar and homely.

But then Toshin disappeared into the bathroom, and reappeared in full uniform with his name tag on. He presented his civilian clothes to

Otto in a folded pile. Otto put them on right there and then. Without being asked, Toshin brought to the table a cup of coffee.

'Let me know,' he said, 'if you need anything else.'

Otto pushed the cup all the way to the other side of the table, dissatisfied.

BABYDOG

I let my boyfriend transform my flat from pigsty to terrarium and he filled it with ferns, succulents, trellises of ivy. So when he told me he'd adopted a new family member I assumed he meant a house plant. Instead, after a long day at work, I found something animal lolling in the hallway. Hairless cushions of skin settled around its neck and stomach. It whined with a juvenile mouth, and its eyes wobbled like poorly-fried eggs. I left the front door open in the hope it might escape, but it dragged its chubby bum across the hardwood floorboards into the kitchen, wanting fed.

—What the hell is this? I asked, on my boyfriend's return.

He'd prepared a speech.

—Pets and queers have a special relationship. They're better than children. You don't have to explain yourself to them. Nobody comes out to their cat, or cockatoo. Their love is unconditional. It'll be good for us. *Instructive.*

I pressed for an explanation of what type of pet it might be.

—*He* is called Alfred. They're a *dog*. Obviously.

There was nothing obvious about it. With no tail to hide between its stubby legs the beast looked like a grub. Its bark sounded like small children at play. Before going outside my boyfriend would press sunblock into its many lumps, as if taking a baby to the beach. I couldn't bear to watch it eat, down on all fours, pale moon-face pressed deep into the bowl, issuing contented grunting noises that were almost human. My boyfriend doted. He spoke to it with a made-up language and, fluent in gibberish, it responded in kind. He carried it down stairs as if worried it might tumble and upon impact with the final step explode like a bleached watermelon.

At night it cried so loud he let it sleep in our bed and once, while we were fucking, it panted by my ear until my boyfriend came. On the occasions when it would eat its own shit, my boyfriend would chortle and call it a *silly billy mucky puppy* while it smeared white turds around its pink lips.

Four months in, I snapped. Over breakfast I made clear there was no room in my life for something so disgusting and dependent. That evening I found the flat empty, but for Alfred sitting in a puddle. A note had been Sellotaped to the gormless thing's bald head.

You need him, the note read, *more than I need you.*

A change of scene: a clinical boardroom in a Tokyo skyscraper, a dozen people in attendance. Almost all are very clever, but only one is very rich, and very unwell. They discuss the company's latest line of transgenic companions, some of which have demonstrated very uncharacteristic expressions. One very clever person suggests the manufacture of these animals was a misstep, albeit profitable, in their search for a cure to the rich person's unwellness. The clever person restates their objections to using dogs as their host organism, and suggests revisiting captivity-bred pygmy elephants; despite heightened rates of rickets, they show greater resistance to the disease, synthesise more antigen, and are less likely to sell on the dark web. The clever person then provides irrefutable proof of what everyone already knows: the very rich person secretly seeded up to eighty percent of the company's fertilized oocytes with strands of his very own DNA, contaminating the new breeds, riddling them with more health concerns than the finest pedigree. Some no longer fit into the milking pods, while others scream in their kennels with half-formed words of loneliness. Worst of all, some specimens were intelligent enough to escape, and have found their way into the public sphere as designer pets. Given how unwell the very rich person is, and how childless, this act of egoism is somewhat understandable, but it risks sinking the entire research project, and so is unforgivable. This very clever person is shown the door and asked to clear their desk by noon. The very rich person thinks in silence for some time, then says:

—Issue a recall. The strays must be destroyed.

*

My jungle house wilted. It took a special kind of care to keep the garden green, an intuition I'd never mastered. I sent my boyfriend a photo of every fern that flopped, every faded ivy, hoping he might provide insights into their taxonomy, and offer resuscitation suggestions. No response.

As for Alfred, I could've tied him to a lamppost on any busy street and walked away, or placed an advert online: *for sale, babydog, never loved*. But I became desensitised to his gulping howls, his sour milky aroma. On weekends and evenings I tried to teach him tricks. I sent my boyfriend videos of our progress. I wanted him to sit up and beg.

On the rare occasion I could be bothered to take Alfred for walks, complete strangers would stop me in the street and inform me he was not natural. I came to see they'd rather missed the point. Alfred filled a need for which mother nature did not suffice. Just in case the poor thing understood what he heard, in a sing-song voice I told him natural selection was nothing to aspire to.

Truth be told, it was a comfort having something living, living with me. But without another human to impress, our standards slipped. The two of us existed, listless, as little more than animals. Alfred would crawl between dirty dishes stacked on the floor next to the sofa, squeeze leftovers between his chubby fingers, and I'd smile at the mess he made, knowing I wasn't likely to clean up after him any time soon. The flat stank of old soil and rot. From home, to habitat.

So Alfred was a comfort, until he wasn't, and one night when even his hapless animal devotion was not enough, I sent a message to my boyfriend: *I need you.*

The next day, my doorbell rang. Was it that easy? Could I bark commands, and be obeyed? Heel, sit, stay? *Sta-a-ay*. Stay. Good boy. Lie down.

But Alfred sat back on his hind legs. He cocked his wrinkled head towards the doorbell's chime. He sniffed the air, and said his first word, deep and clear and fearful:

—Daddy?

ASTERION

PROLOGUE α

These days children run towards the Minotaur. He wears a tidy hat like a sailboat and drives a bright white chariot, with a giant plastic lollipop on top. It plays a double-time version of *The Entertainer*. It also plays *Pop Goes the Weasel,* but something about that particular tune unsettles him. Filling the toppings dispenser, the Minotaur pauses to flick a summer bluebottle from his snout with his tongue. The most lucrative spot during summer is the skate park. He serves swirls with flakes, fruit slushies and screwballs, long fizzy drinks to sip in the grass. Sometimes when it's quiet he'll smoke with the skaters behind the van. He's convinced there's a secret wager over who'll be first to touch his horns. There are a few who, were they older, or he much younger, they would only need to ask politely. Today it's so hot even the self-conscious boys have thrown their baggy tees under trees, while the self-conscious girls keep to the shade. He wears an electronic ankle bracelet connected to a registry downtown because he's still not sure if the sound of children screaming makes him feel hungry or angry. Parents order ices for their children, and sometimes their children cry, and the parents tell them to stop or the bad man will get them. The Minotaur is almost always the bad man in question. He looks the part; by mid-afternoon he smells the part, too. 'Two ice creams, please,' says the next guy in line. The Minotaur, on autopilot, expertly pumps out two Mr Softees. The customer pays but doesn't go anywhere. He waits until the Minotaur actually looks at him. Olive skinned, sculpted curls, nice smile. He hands one cone back with a wink. 'This one's for you.'

He's not one of the self-conscious boys.

PROLOGUE β

Pets are forbidden, but there's musk all through the close. Not poodle nor little terrier nor any city breed; more of a hound-smell, a hunt-smell. Lucille scrunches her nose as she climbs the stairs, although it's not altogether an unenjoyable aroma. A loyal stink, it pads alongside as she opens her front door. When she sits down, she can feel the weight of its head in her lap. Some time later the doorbell rings. She turns on lights and the television before answering. It's the owner of the smell and her new upstairs neighbour, the Minotaur, bringing ingratiating gifts of sea salt and deli olives. A damaged part of her has been falling in love with the most hopeless of men, the passive drunks stuffed into the dark corners of bars, the loners spending hours on the same park bench day after day. She usually shrugs off the impulse and goes home alone, well aware she's projecting onto them a romantic desperation which they've long ago left behind. But there's no fighting it this time. Check out his eyes! So big and sad! He must be so lonely! All those years, all those centuries, with nobody alike in the entire world. Oh sure, he's got a history, but so does everyone. What sentimental fate that two people so sad should find each other!

Lucille invites him in, smitten.

STICHOMYTHIA

After a week of laying low, the Minotaur caves, and calls Damon, even if he doesn't quite know what to say. Not even a hello—he just leaves Damon hanging on the other end.

'Min, are you there?' Damon asks, even though the Minotaur knows he knows the Minotaur must be. Tiny mobiles don't agree with the shape of the Minotaur's head, so instead he has this big Bakelite thing that occupies his bedside table, always set to speaker-phone. He sits on his bed, surrounded by dusty pictures unearthed by a fit of spring cleaning. So many are portraits of himself, you'd think he was a narcissist. Framed digital prints, loose disposables from the 90s, daguerreotypes, scratchy cubist things, a few charcoal rubbings of crumbling old walls.

The most recent is a Polaroid of him and Damon posing in Speedos on Pefkos beach. They each look so happy, they might as well be strangers.

'I feel like I need to apologise,' says Damon. 'The way we left it.'

Such a kind euphemism to describe last week's tryst. The Minotaur's heart swells with appreciation, but something's off. Why isn't Damon angry? Why did he even pick up the call? It would be reasonable for him to never want to see The Minotaur again, the way they *left it*.

'Are you doing anything right now? It's a nice day. We could grab a coffee. It would be nice to see you.'

The Minotaur snorts, and Damon hangs up. From the Polaroid, their past selves grin as if nothing will ever hurt them. The Minotaur can almost feel hot sand underfoot, salt crusting on his hairy back. He plays with his nose ring, a nervous tic. His horns were sharper, then.

Lucille spends the morning watching her bedroom's bare light bulb dance to the beat of the Minotaur's footsteps. Partly by osmosis, partly through obsession, she has figured out most of his routines. She will sometimes move with him from one room to another to prove to herself how well she knows him. Totally normal neighbourly behaviour. But this week has been unusual. He's paced, stamped, sometimes stood at his front door without leaving.

Now, however, he's going through to the bathroom, running a tap while he brushes his teeth, then to the kitchen where he gets a glass of water, and then once more back to the bathroom to urinate. This is his leaving-the-house routine. After he's gone, she moves into the stairwell and makes a half-jump to reach the ledge where he hides his spare key. The Minotaur locks himself out more often than most. It's a psychological issue. She likes to read about psychotherapy, and while she doesn't fully understand Freud's fixation on Medusa, she likes his theories on how forgetting is really a function of your subconscious. Your psyche seeks out reasons to return, says Freud. She has her own theories about why the Minotaur so often locks himself out. Well, she calls them theories. Theoretical purists would claim they're more akin to fantasies.

Almost as often as he locks himself out, Lucille lets herself in.

*

The cafe rumbles golden with spring sun through the skylight. The Minotaur sits with his back to the door. The tables are small and round, set with blue tulips in tall milk jugs and thin china plates twice as wide as the food. They had their first date over by the window, where the Minotaur made Damon laugh by being clumsy. The Minotaur suspects he's to provide similar comic relief today but, still very much on the defensive, he concentrates on moving delicately.

'I'm surprised you brought the van,' says Damon. The skin around his left eye still bears discolouration, a bruised eclipse.

It's February, who buys ice cream in winter? But the more they make a sport of looking away from each other, the more he fancies a quick, melodic getaway.

The waitress brings Damon's pomegranate salad and the Minotaur's bowl of tofu; the one thing he still likes about this place is that it caters to speciality diets. The Minotaur eats as quietly as his bovine head will allow.

'So… about last week.'

The Minotaur has no tees or jumpers for obvious reasons. His taste in cardigans and shirts tends towards the neutrals, the sandstones and greys of his childhood home. Lucille chokes down another dose of beta blockers and inhales from the Minotaur's size thirty-sixes. Jeans are tailored for his rather big thighs; Lucille likes to lie down with them on the bed, her head resting near the crotch, imagining the smell of his flesh through the denim But not today. His bed is occupied by memories that go beyond her. Dust settles on the photos. For the first time since the first time, she feels like an intruder.

'He's a *minotaur*. Aren't they lusty? Hungry? Lonely?'

She says it out loud, as if it might scare away the idea that he may be all of the above, only never for her, as if the young man in the beach photo might overhear and bury himself in the sand, as if there were ever other minotaur, and multiple choice studies charting their loneliness on a sliding scale between 'not at all' and 'most definitely.'

On the precipice of an epiphany as to what the Minotaur's singular nature portends with regards to his compatibility with humanity, the pills grab the collar of her coat before she can flutter off the edge.

Last week was the first time they'd met since the break-up a year previous. Filling each other in on life events, an evening walk through the park had strayed into the cruising area, the river path dotted with men anticipating dusk. The Minotaur had tried cruising, once—it's a wink in the roses, a long hard stare across shrubs—but without the blessing of anonymity it seemed a bit futile. Damon took this admission as a challenge and, ever the willing champion, grabbed the Minotaur's wrist and threaded him through the trees. All too late, he understood where he was being led. The hedge maze.

Damon had meant the best. To lead him there was to say open secrets yet unspoken could be left to the side to have sediment of days heaped upon them until they turned to myth. The Minotaur understood this. But the man's fear had filled his wet nose. Memories sprang from the bushes, sharp like holly in a glory hole. A black sail wrapped around the rising moon.

'You don't remember any of this?' Damon picks at his pomegranate salad, appetite waning. 'The park? The fight?'

The Minotaur recalls the blackout coming on and nothing more, although he suspects it went further than simple violence—Damon has kinks, obviously, to be fooling around with him. The only reason the Minotaur from outright assuming they fucked that night is the fact he hasn't remembered any fucking in, oh, a few thousand years or so.

Is drag an option? Lucille goes to the Minotaur's bathroom, which is a horror show, fur clogging the sink plughole, toothpaste crusting on a hairbrush, a mirror spattered with the dried ghosts of early morning sneezes. She looks past the streaks of old mucus to scrutinise her face. It's soft. It looks like it should be malleable, like she should be able to press it like clay until cheekbones break through. A pencilled beard would be unconvincing, but a jar of Vaseline and a split teabag could pass for stubble. She could dress like him and be her own wooden cow. Shoulders set far back, Lucille tries to look hard and hollow and ready to breed.

The man in the photos doesn't look hard, though. Somewhat gallant, thoughtful, like he'd suit both youth and old age, but not cope so great between the two. Perhaps the Minotaur likes them lost, she thinks.

'Can I change the tune?' Damon asks as they pull into a petrol station. The Minotaur shrugs and, once parked, digs the van's manual out from the glove compartment. It lands in Damon's lap with a puff of stale air, and Damon flips through it while the Minotaur fills the tank. The chimes pages are a mess of scores, most of the animal-themed ones scratched with such a heavy hand the page is torn. A dozen or so of the others remain legible. The current tune, *The Entertainer* is honoured with an asterix next to it, as is *Girls and Boys (Come Out To Play)*.

'Is this one as creepy as it sounds?'

The Minotaur shrugs. Damon shuffles over to the driver's seat window to get a good look at the Minotaur.

'If you don't want to do this...'

The Minotaur slaps the cap shut and hooks the pump.

'Fine, I'll stop asking, but you're being childish.'

Nobody glares quite like an angry bull with two millennia of practice.

'No,' says Alex. 'I don't care how long you've been kicking about, you *are* being childish. I'm trying to help you in spite of everything, so hear me out. What happened in the maze, it's not as simple as forgiving and forgetting, and anyway that's impossible, you can't do both. Forgetting's instant, it's gone. Forgiving takes constant work, you have to remember something before you can forgive it, and you have to remember you forgave it, and why, and then you've to remember to forgive it again. It's continual. You've been around so long, you've become lazy. You think anger's the way out. It's the easiest, yeah, but it's not the only way.'

The Minotaur would disagree. Each and every blackout is difficult, a dead end, a return to a centre he can't escape. But it's been a long time since anyone's cared enough to follow him into the dark.

20

*

Classically conditioned, Lucille's trained herself to leave the Minotaur's flat when she hears *The Entertainer* blaring its way back towards their block. They live in a quiet area of town and she'll realise she's been paying attention to the song halfway through putting his things back where she found them. By the time the Minotaur's parking outside she's already half-jumping to put his key back on the ledge in the close. But this only works with *The Entertainer*. The nursery chant of *Girls and Boys* doesn't even register, so she's still trying to decide which of his shirts make her look more masculine when she hears the Minotaur's keys in the lock.

Should she hide? He's brought somebody home. Lucille feels more horrified at the thought of being caught snooping by a stranger than by the Minotaur himself. The bathroom is out of the question as she'd have to pass them in the hallway. She's not jumping out a third floor window, as there's no romance in such an embarrassing death. Under the bed? No, just... no. She doesn't remember ever being this panicked in her fantasies. Oh, the Minotaur is hungry, lonely, lusty, yes, but angry, sharp and territorial too. And real. Most monstrous of all, he's real.

Lucille, draped in borrowed threads, climbs into the Minotaur's wardrobe.

Cattle can detect odours up to five miles away. Considering Lucille's been leaving her scent on everything for months now, a wardrobe is child's play

Damon sits on the Minotaur's bed and sifts through the Pefkos beach Polaroids, then the charcoals, then the blocky etchings. He recognises them, then starts to laugh, and says, 'I shouldn't be surprised. Of course this was you. Made you look good, too. Very manly.'

The Minotaur wonders if Damon's thinking of the other, bigger, more famous Picassos where he's straddling naked women; there are some with men, too, but never exclusively so. There is one with a child. The brace on his ankle grows heavy. He avoids the art scene now; it is too permissive and, at any rate, he no longer requires their skills to keep track of how the world sees him. Amateurs can prop their camera on a rock, set a timer, pose with him on the sand, and it is no less representative. The idea of a self-portrait worries him. He packs the pictures back into their boxes with a closer eye to organisation than usual. Damon watches with patience and a smirk. With his broad back to the bed, The Minotaur opens the wardrobe door halfway and, crouching to eye level with Lucille, places the pictures at her feet. The Picasso sits atop the pile. He nudges it towards her and she takes it, wild-eyed, silent.

'Quit stalling,' says Damon, ever the romantic.

The Minotaur shuts Lucille in.

Through a gap between the doors, Lucille watches as Damon rises to meet the Minotaur. Held at the waist, he rests his head against the Minotaur's thick neck; with delicate movements he nudges deep into the Minotaur's mane, where Lucille hears him inhale soft and slow.

'If you feel yourself drifting,' he says, 'let me know. We'll stop, and we'll pick up again when you come back.'

The Minotaur nods and walks him back towards the bed. Damon sits down and holds the backs of the Minotaur's knees, presses his face against the Minotaur's belly. The Minotaur starts to undo his belt, but Damon lifts the big hands away and holds them out to the side.

'Nuh-uh. Slower.'

Damon shuffles backwards and the Minotaur kneels up on the bed. When the Minotaur bends down to kiss, his tongue is rough and grey in Damon's mouth. Damon hooks one hand in the Minotaur's jeans, with the other rubs behind one goofy oval ear. It looks, to Lucille, as if the Minotaur likes it, but he shakes his head free and snorts. The labyrinth is creeping up on him.

'Eyes open, Min.'

Damon holds the Minotaur's gaze until the man half returns. Gripping horns Damon draws the heavy body down to lying prone. Lucille can see Damon's legs and chin and lips sticking out from under the Minotaur. An arm wriggles free and reaches towards the Minotaur's crotch; the Minotaur lows. It sets Lucille's teeth on edge. They hold still like this for quite some time, until Damon complains of a lack of circulation in his feet. More untangling, and the shirt, the shoes, the jeans come off. The ankle tag stays on. The Minotaur's back and belly are hairier than Lucille expects, his build fatter, more bullish. It's a bulk made for bursts of brutal force, but Damon's constant whisperings keep it calm and slow.

In the shadows of the wardrobe she can just about discern the details of the Picasso etching. He's singular, yes; alone, perhaps; but the charcoals, the oil paintings, the chips of marble in a box, they're one unbroken chain of infatuation as long as history itself. Like a lance to the head, it strikes Lucille that the Minotaur has never been *lonely*. How could he ever be lonely? Ever since the very first sunrise, there's always been someone to wipe their own blood off his snout and finger-paint his children on the walls.

Sitting triumphantly on Damon's chest, the Minotaur whips off his underwear. His ass is crowned by the scarred nub of a clumsily docked tail. Like a curse lifted, she doesn't find him, him the beast, him the total sum of man and bull, in any way attractive. He's still functional, and such a terrible function at that—she would like to be his red rag, his ankle tag, his gored toreador—but despite daily practise, she cannot imagine herself in that bed nor recognise this gentle version of the beast, even as she watches it be tamed. Drained of expectations, she's tired. Her calves are cramping. She waits for a particularly noisy moo to cover her manoeuvre into a more comfortable position, and beds down among the Minotaur's clothes.

Waiting on the darkness of sleep, she makes a promise to herself: no more ritual visits.

EPILOGUE

Summer is on its way again, and the Minotaur is back at his spot, slinging raspberry swirls. He's considering quitting the trade—with Damon's help navigating dark orridors of memory, grief and guilt, it has become obvious to the Minotaur that children really do just make him angry. The mere thought of the little brats fills him with wanderlust. Today, though, it's quiet by the skate park, and he's leaning against the back of the van smoking. There's something hypnotic about the constant movement of the skaters, the back and forth and back around again. Used to be a time, long ago, when he would have lowered his head and charged the lot of them, but not now.

He's been watching this one girl, a regular, sail round the concrete for the last two hours or so. She wears a long denim shirt like a dress, and a small backpack which pulls the shirt tight around her chest. Every so often a guy will keep pace with her and sometimes she'll flirt back. If she really likes a guy she'll unzip the backpack and show off the spray cans inside.

This one guy, after he's seen the cans, not-so-surreptitiously points towards the Minotaur. She circles the park a few times before summoning the courage to approach him.

'Hey, um,' she says. 'Can I bum a smoke?'

The Minotaur obliges, though he knows she doesn't smoke. She tucks the cigarette in her back pocket and squints up at him.

'So, like, don't look, but my friend he thinks I won't… god, this is so embarrassing. If it's really personal forget it. I want to impress him and… yeah. Could I, like, do a picture of you, on the park? Over there by the grindrail. You're here, like, all the time. Some of the guys have said you're thinking of leaving, and that makes me sorta sad. I want to, you know, commemorate or something. Just a picture, if you don't mind much.'

The Minotaur doesn't mind at all.

MOUTHFEEL

Nathan located the restaurant on the corner of Kent Road and Berkeley Street: another hasty pop-up in the race to gentrify Finnieston, it bore no signage, no menu board. The only guarantee of a hot dinner was Lizzie, standing by a blank door in her favourite red polka dot dress. She waved at him across the street, and pointed to her watch. As Nathan waited for a gap in the traffic, a sharp sensation of chives appeared unbidden in his mouth—serving as an early warning of the Stilton, which arrived more blue than cheese. He slipped a bottle of mouthwash from his coat pocket, swilled a quick mouthful and spat into the gutter.

'I saw that,' Lizzie said as he approached. He kissed her on the cheek as a greeting. 'Minty fresh, as always.' She touched her pearl earring to make sure he hadn't dislodged it, then looked him over. 'Oh Nate, trainers? What did I tell you about looking smart? You'll be lucky not to be turned away, this is an exclusive opening.'

'This isn't smart?' Nathan his wrinkled shirt into his jeans and zipped up his jacket. 'There, nobody can tell I'm a big old scruff.'

'Everyone will be able to tell, Nathan,' said Lizzie. 'They're rich. Give me your hand, if we pretend we're an item they might not notice.'

Lizzie pulled him to the door. He'd not seen her this excited in a long time, although that was more his fault than anything else. Too many hours spent in the office fiddling with lines of code for clients whose concepts of deadlines were incompatable with a social life.

'Surprised you asked me along,' he said. 'Not really my sort of thing.'

'I wasn't about to show up to a tasting night solo, was I? Anyway, I've been worried about you. Man cannot live on Soylent alone.'

'Actually,' said Nathan, 'I think that's the point.'

'Humour me, will you?' She squeezed his shoulder. 'Just for tonight, leave your curious condition at the door?'

This was Nathan's condition: his mouth had forever been haunted by the ghosts of meals he hadn't eaten. Foods he didn't even like—liquorice, coffee, anything with strawberry flavouring—made frequent appearances, despite attempts to avoid them in person. Some flavours went through phases. A week of high-grade sushi. A month of hospital food, aggressively beige. His twenties had been characterised by the bubbled saltiness of caviar manifesting each Hogmanay, though it wasn't until his thirtieth birthday Nathan got the chance to connect the taste to its real-world counterpart, at a restaurant not unlike this one. Other times, the phantom flavours interrupted meals he was already eating, muddying the entire experience. Christmas in particular was unpleasant, like sucking on a chocolate-covered stock cube.

He had a theory. His mouth, somehow, was connected to another. Telepathy of the tongue. He'd shared this theory once with Lizzie, who'd called him organic, free-range bonkers and refused to entertain the idea any further. Yet other sensations could not originate from food. A frequent probing warm wetness, for example, begun at sixteen, bloomed at night into a sticky, salty suddenness. He knew what that was. Unmistakable. Personally, Nathan preferred to spit, but to each their own.

Going down, stairs led to a basement, the decor sitting somewhere between a New York speakeasy and a half-finished public restroom. Typical for the area. A young man showed them to their table. Once seated, Nathan was hit by another imaginary wave of Stilton, this time accompanied by a light mouthfeel of something melting on his tongue.

Mouthwash was one of his coping methods, the intensity of peppermint enough to banish even the most stubborn spirits. The invention of Soylent—a lab-brewed dust-flavoured meal-in-a-sachet—had been something of a blessing, as it cut out all interference. But as their waitress provided a small wooden board laid with four canapes: blue stilton and chives on a buttermilk wafer, Nathan realised, there would be no interference tonight.

By the bar, a wine glass and teaspoon commanded attention. A large man in a three piece suit beamed at his guests, paired with a round-shouldered chef, her height almost matching his, if you included her toque. Together they delivered some guff about pushing boundaries and contributing to the neighbourhood's legacy for experimental dining. Nathan didn't hear a word. He was too dumbfounded by the serendipity of canapes.

'He's here,' breathed Nathan.

'Who?'

'My other taster.'

'I don't want to talk about it, Nathan. Look, here comes our food.'

Matched with a slim glass of Chardonnay boasting notes of pineapple over buttered toast, the first course was a bisque of langoustine with white chocolate and garlic. Nathan pushed it around with his spoon.

'They know what they're doing,' said Lizzie. Nathan pinched his nose in preparation. Lizzie reached across the table and slapped his hand. 'Stop embarassing me. Just try it. Please.'

So he did. The crustacean wash gave way to a sweet cream on the way down, at once seaside and farmyard, sending his brain into a strange pinching pleasure.

'See?' Lizzie said, as his eyes grew wide. 'You're missing out.'

The sensation of hot, smooth bisque filled Nathan's mouth again. Not an after-taste. First contact, twice. Then came the wine. At least, he assumed it was the wine, though his palate wasn't refined enough to identify anything as exact as pineapple. But he'd not touched his Chardonnay, the fine glass as yet unsmudged by fingerprints.

As they ate and chatted about their days, he couldn't shake the feeling that someone he'd never been sure existed, but had known intimately throughout his life, was now here with them, hidden among strangers.

'Recognise anyone?' he asked Lizzie.

'Oh, the usual crowd. Press and foodies.' She looked at him with a sigh. 'Can't we play Guess Who later? I'm right here, Nate. I haven't seen you in months. Since you started on that liquid goop you don't eat like normal people.'

'You've got it the wrong way round. I don't eat like normal people, that's why I'm on that liquid goop in the first place—you know that.'

Their second course arrived. The venison haunch was obvious enough, sitting medium-rare at one end of the bamboo board, but the sweet potato puree, caramelised chestnuts, gingerbread crumble and spiced roast plum were abstracted in dots and blobs, closer to modern art than food. Nathan hovered his fork first over one element, then the other, unsure of where to start. Lizzie rolled her eyes. As they ate, Nathan peered at the other diners. Was anyone shocked when he took a fluffy mouthful of crumble, or a rich cut of venison? Every flavour on the board blended with its neighbours. The puree gifted the plum a constancy of texture, its sweetness taking centre-stage when paired with the woody chestnuts. The crumble stole the venison's juice, the plums returned the moistness. Nathan found if he alternated medleyed mouthfuls with his invisible dining companion, he could create a constant, shifting gradient of tastes and textures, as if he'd bitten out a chunk out of the Northern Lights.

'I have to meet them,' he said, half-standing to look around the dim-lit restaurant. Was there a flicker of interest from the thin, eagle-faced man alone in the corner by the door? Or the two elderly women sitting near the bar? What about the table of young party animals whose shiny helium birthday balloon bobbed against the ceiling? Did any of them seem curious?

'Good grief.' Lizzie downed her wine. 'You should've stood me up, at least then I'd get double portions.'

Nathan slumped back into his seat. Double portions. Triple portions. Centuple portions. His telepathic tongue could be linked to every mouth in the room and he'd never know Eve from Adam, all of them eating the same apple.

Unless he went off-menu.

'Don't judge, okay?' He lifted Lizzie's empty wine glass. 'This is a test.'

'This whole night is a fucking test, if you ask me.'

Under the table, Nathan took his bottle of mouthwash and sloshed some into the glass. The chemical scent was alarming, out of place.

'Nate. I told you, put it away.'

He tipped the whole lot into his mouth—

'Nathan!'

—and held it there. Two round cheekfuls of dental cleaning fluid. Their waitress approached, concerned. 'Sir, are you okay?'

Nathan nodded, and tried to smile without dribbling. Lizzie, less courteous, waved the waitress away, mortified. His eyes watered, his sinuses flamed, the menthol tingle flayed his taste buds in waves. But he didn't desist.

'Augh!'

The eagle-faced man in the corner leapt to his feet, knocking his chair to the wooden floor. He pushed his way to the bathroom, a hand over his mouth. Nathan spat the mouthwash back into Lizzie's glass and took a strong gulp of white wine from his own. Under the soothing grape twisted sour by the mint, he felt tap water bubbling against the back of his throat, a cleansing gargle.

'Give me that.' Lizzie snatched her glass away and marched to the ladies' room, returning to the table empty-handed. Nathan began to apologise, but stopped. Lizzie was looking at him funny.

'That's Eugene Richmond,' she said. 'You know Margot Richmond? Three Star Michelin Matriarch of Paris? I guess not. Rumour has it, she's written him out of her will. He's incompetent, she's tried to teach him everything she knows, but it just won't stick. She doesn't want him near her empire. So of course he became a critic. But he couldn't even get that right. His reviews were unusual, sometimes perfect but sometimes flat out wrong. Nobody took him seriously until...' Lizzie leaned back in her chair and covered her mouth. 'When did you start using Soylent?'

'About two years ago? Two and a half?'

'And it tastes of...?'

'Nothing, really.'

'Aye. That's when Eugene got his book deal. Everyone assumed he'd hired a ghost-writer.'

Chatter rose around them as Eugene Richmond exited the men's room and began collecting his belongings.

'Don't just sit there,' hissed Lizzie. 'Go talk to him! Butter him up! Get us an invitation to his mum's flagship!'

She didn't have to tell Nathan twice. He dodged his way to the stairwell through a flurry of servers carrying plates of star fruit coconut cheesecake, its layers de-constructed into poetry. He brushed past the doorman. Eugene was almost out on the street, almost gone.

Words came to Nathan in a rush:

'What do you taste like?'

Eugene Richmond paused on the top stair, facing out into the night, one step from disconnection.

'Excuse me?'

'That came out wrong. I mean...'

Nathan wondered if at this moment Eugene's mouth was also dry.

'What is taste like, for you?'

Nathan tasted vomit. Eugene braced himself against the door frame.

'It's you, isn't it?'

One hallucinogenic dessert later, the kitchen was closed, but Eugene had bribed the round-shouldered chef to knock up a feast of small plates, promising his first ever five-star review. Lizzie stayed behind also, to make amends to the staff with some very expensive champagne, which she had for no good reason started calling 'bubbly', something she'd never done before.

Over this private banquet, Eugene and Nathan came to understand some of their more unusual, unexplained experiences. A soggy scuttling sensation in Eugene's childhood, the memory of which gave him nightmares to this day, had come from when Nathan, under a dare, had placed a beetle inside his mouth, panicked, and bit down. Meanwhile, a year of burnt pepperoni had, in fact, been the taste of Eugene's chain-smoking ex-boyfriend, kissing.

'Allow me to try something?' said Eugene. He was quite handsome when he smiled, the severity of his birdlike nose softened by a lopsided pair of dimples. 'Close your eyes.'

Nathan did so, and felt a cool lightness on his tongue, a woodsy caramel flavour that melted down the sides, tart and savoury and sweet at once.

'Parsnip?' Nathan guessed. 'But charred and runny. The frothy stuff.'

'The mousse, exactement!'

When Nathan opened his eyes, Eugene had lifted his glass of

champagne, and motioned for Nathan to do the same. They both sipped, then smiled. It was impossible to tell where one man's experience came to a close, and the other began anew.

'Not once did I ever enjoy a meal the way I knew I was meant to,' said Eugene, 'Until tonight. It feels less... lonely, no?'

Decades running parallel to each other, but connected, two paths meeting in an impossible space. Now here they were, feeling altogether more-ish, umami for the soul. Nathan laughed. Eugene was right. *Exactement.*

He scooped up the last remaining mouthful of cheesecake, and shared it with him.

WHEN ALL WE'VE LOST
IS FOUND AGAIN

The same night Rob is due to fly out, the *Florentine* disappears. A coincidence, that's all. There's no meaning to it. Even so, Declan can't help but think of it as an omen as he drives Rob to the airport. When they leave the suburbs behind and enter the deep countryside, the world exists only where the headlights touch the tarmac of the winding road.

Declan motions to the tablet sitting on top of the dashboard. 'Check if there's any news yet.'

'They'd text me if the flight was cancelled.'

'I mean about the *Florentine*.'

Rob leans forward in the passenger seat, not to check the tablet but to look up at the night sky. Declan glances over to admire the line of his shaved head, his long nose, his Adam's apple; like the road, his boyfriend seems only to exist where the light touches his face. Then the car hits a bump, too fast, and Rob's thrown back in his seat.

'If I'd known you were this anxious,' Rob sighs, 'I'd have taken the bus. Are the thousands other people flying out today similarly doomed? Or am I special?'

'You're special to me,' Declan says.

'But not so special that you want to come along?'

Declan almost misses the turn that leads to the airport car park. A reckless change of lane. Rob grips the dashboard and goes quiet. Good. They've argued this point many times and Declan isn't interested in retreading old ground. A year spent travelling the world is a throwaway sort of dream, an adventure for folk who, whether through luxury or bad luck, have nothing left to lose but time and money. They're both well past the point in their lives. That's what Declan believes, at any rate. He can see the appeal, of course he can. Compared to his admin job at the heritage museum, Rob's day job as a hospital porter is easier to leave behind. But the timing is atrocious. After such a stressful period trying to buy their new home, Declan's still having nightmares of ink-resistant mortgage forms, and doors with locks that when you look closer are actually smaller doors, with tiny locks that upon inspection reveal themselves as even *smaller* doors, and so on. If Declan went along with Rob's gallivanting then he'd have no choice but to devote what little is left of his savings to the adventure, and so there would be less chance of the trip ending prematurely, but then also there's the house, they'd have to sell the inessential stuff and put the rest in storage. There'd be nothing to come back to, they'd have to start over. And the garden! He had such plans for the garden, everything tagged in rows and plots, maintained and neat and proper. So much would be squandered, or abandoned. No. Declan won't have it. They haven't yet settled. After years of pressing the soft clay of their lives together, this new sculpture is still unfinished, a clay mould without the plaster. After years of work, Rob wants to start a new project? Declan refuses to entertain the idea. Some hopes must be lived-in before you make space for new ones.

'That wasn't a rhetorical question,' Rob says as they pull into the airport parking lot. It takes Declan a moment to remember what he asked.

'You're special enough to me that I'll hold everything in place while you get this wanderlust out of your system.'

'That doesn't sound as romantic as you think it does,' says Rob, but there's a smile in his voice.

They both feel silly for crying at gate security, and kiss hard, though Rob dislikes public displays, and they promise to send each other a picture every day. Then it's a three minute sprint back through the shopping area and out past the drop-off point to the car park, where Declan sits in the car, face lit in the dark by the light of the tablet, as he tries to find information on the *Florentine*.

Declan had only ever been casually interested in cosmology. Like many, his curiosity stretched to Mars and no further, unless his horoscope was particularly uncanny. But that was before NASA discovered the rift in the wall of the universe, which they did by accident, by losing a satellite with an unmemorable name made of numbers. One moment it was out there in outer space, verifiable; the next, nowhere, uncommunicative. It reappeared somewhere new that was neither. For seventeen seconds the satellite broadcast readings that made no sense, fed back data that made the universe a stranger to Newton and Einstein, until it crashed into something in the dark and was lost again, this time forever.

Tonight's loss of the *Florentine*, however, is deliberate. The two-billion pound probe was launched on an identical trajectory, with no guarantee it might follow the misplaced satellite into this odd middling place. Such expensive and wilful negligence, married to such mystery, sparked a public frenzy of interest, of which Rob seemed to be the only one immune. Even as late as last week, lying in bed together and browsing an online catalogue of bathroom furnishings, Rob had been baffled as to why so many bathmats and shower curtains were space-themed, swirling with planets and rocket ships. After some deliberation they settled on a lime green toothbrush holder to go with the towels that came with the house.

Now, sitting in the car alone, Declan's obsessive search for news on the Florentine is interruped by a notification banner across the tablet's screen: *day one! the journey of a lifetime begins with a single seat by the window kiss kiss love you loads.* Attached is a picture of the airport as seen from inside the aeroplane. Declan stares at the notification until it disappears like dotted lines in the rear view mirror.

There is no fresh news. The nine hour communication delay from the *Florentine* means there will be no information until the morning. Even still, as Declan drives home, he reaches over from the steering wheel and taps the screen to refresh, refresh, refresh.

The updates, when they come, set the world on standby. At the heritage museum, nobody does any work. Not that there's much work to do. The manor and its artworks are low maintenance. Everything is in its place.

The same cannot be said for what's beyond the rift. The first object the *Florentine* discovers is its predecessor, the dead satellite compacted into the side of a Ford Fiesta which, once the license plates are identified, was reported missing in 1986. The car, Declan marvels, disappeared the same summer he was born. Caught shiny and sterile in the *Florentine's* camera flash, both the Fiesta and the satellite hang unmoving in the void like bubbles trapped in dark amber. NASA try to explain the crashed satellite's loss of momentum, but they're as unable to explain the absence of the laws of motion in this place, as they are the presence of literally everything else they find. The *Florentine* streams footage as it moves, searchlights sweeping slow and steady through the flat black space. All around it is junk. Cracked ballpoint pens, hair clips, dull pennies of every currency. White specks which appear to be far-off galaxies reveal themselves as several buttons, almost adjacent to the camera and out-of-focus. Someone orders the *Florentine* to turn 180 degrees and a white blur fills the screen. A sea of buttons, billions of them. Clusters of small white buttons of varying sizes. Some still with thread attached.

day two! this hotel room is lush! wish you were here to help ruin the sheets ;D

Declan has no reply, but he taps out a polite *haha me too*. He's never liked strange beds, in unfamiliar rooms, walls adorned with inoffensive art, people paid to sneak in after you've gone out for the day and fix everything, so when you return it's good as new, like you were never there. There was a chaotic sort of reassurance in mess.

Lost Space. That's what everyone calls it after the *Florentine* finds the Baychimo. The ship, a cargo steamer over a century old, floats vertically in the void. Its masts and chimney seem unusually long when viewed horizontally. Or perhaps that's only down to how the *Florentine* approaches it.

day five! noodles for one!

never mind, found a friend

The background is too dark to discern what sort of noodle bar lets patrons eat in leather harnesses. He's not Rob's type, this new pal. Beefier and hairier and more into kink than Rob likes, or at least more than Declan thought Rob liked. Is day five too early for revelations?

andre wants to know where your picture is, you haven't sent me one today

With the mental equivalent of a shrug Declan sends a screenshot of the *Florentine's* newest and oddest find. The machine is a clear beaker with a nipple-shaped top, with tubes both black and clear running to a metal canister that splits into four plungers connected at a complex intersection. Because everything in the *Florentine*'s photos appears flat against the solid black background, it's impossible to guess at the scale of the contraption.

andre says he wishes you were here to use it on him

Declan considers whether ot not to play along, decides against it, and replies: *I'm not sure it's meant for humans.*

Declan doesn't hear from Rob for the rest of the night.

Autumn turns to winter with a cold snap of the fingers. Footfall at the heritage museum drops to an all-time low. Seasonal fluctuations are the norm for tourist attractions, but this year their competition is stiff. All of history's mysteries, accessible via an online portal; of course nobody wants to visits a museum. NASA hires some Silicon Valley geniuses to automate the *Florentine*'s live feed, so that it only captures images of things it hasn't seen before. Gone are the thousands of pictures of single socks and handbags, the rubber ducks and wristwatches. Now it only collects oddities, historical items and works of art. It uploads them to a public database. Scientists are not as well versed in the humanities as all of humanity put together, and so they crowdsource a catalogue of everything mankind has ever waylaid. Most of it is depressing garbage but some of it is curious. Abstract sculptures made out of unidentifiable rock, their surface puckered as if vacuum-packed. They must be contemporary but nobody in the art world claims them, even as the collection expands to contain hundreds of the things. Perhaps they're the work of some artist in a shack in the Arizona desert who died before anyone from the art world could 'discover' them.

There's a substantial cash prize for whoever finds the real Florentine Diamond, the probe's namesake. It's a fingernail sized gem cut from lemon-lime stone in the sixteenth century which was misplaced, in the grand scheme of things, almost immediately. Caught in the probe's spotlight against the uniform black of Lost Space, it will show as bright as a distant supernova.

How would you spend the money?

Seen two days ago.

Declan knows how Rob would spend the money—not on toothbrush holders or new bedsheets, that's for sure—but he wants to send something that merits a response. Because as the dark of winter sets in, Rob stops communicating. Declan would worry if the messages he sent bounced back or were left unread. If all this time he'd been sending carrier pigeons across the whole wide world only for them to slap up against a closed window and fall away. But they're getting through, Rob is reading the messages, the app says so.

Rather than worry, Declan sinks hours into cataloguing for the *Florentine*. It's time he'd otherwise spend following Rob around the internet, drawing invisible string between strangers in the background of profile pictures, and new followers, and likes and comments and those little animated hearts Declan knows Rob hates. Only Rob likes them now. He's changing. On nights when Declan has the *Florentine*'s feed open in one laptop window and Rob's social media open in another, scrolling into dawn feeling equal parts raw and infinitesimal, the two worlds blend together. A trail of blurry pictures taken in the sorts of dive bars they used to avoid. A collection of striped bendy straws. A video of Rob doing karaoke in a neon lit booth, surrounded by men in much neater suits than his own rented affair. A used colostomy bag. The cephalopod stares at him from inside a lavender bubble. Over weeks Rob grows out his beard against a backdrop of big rocks and cacti. A bowling ball engraved in Arabic. The beard vanishes and Declan mourns never finding out what it's like to kiss him when he tastes of argan oil and sand.

Wait, what the *fuck?*

Scroll back.

The cephalopod stares at him from inside a lavender bubble.

Like the many arms of the Vetruvian Man, its tentacles press up against the sides of the sphere, revealing row after row of oily suckers. The obscene proportions of its bulbous head narrow into a birdlike beak. Tubes protrude from the beak and wrap around its abdomen, other ends attached to apparatus harnessed to the ceiling of the bubble. It has to be an animatronic, a special effect from the golden age of scifi, that slipped into the shadows at the back of a Hollywood warehouse.

Have you seen this?

Seen two minutes ago.

Rob? Are you there?

Seen a moment ago.

I know you're there. Please. Look at the pic and talk to me about it.

No response. Oh well, Declan tells himself.;in the big scheme of things, which now includes a pocket dimension populated by trash and a squid trapped inside a purple disc, a long-term boyfriend going incommunicado isn't as meaningful as it might once have been. Or so he wants to believe.

The *Florentine* Project provides no means of reporting something this unexpected. He can tag it as 'Unknown' and move on, but assigning it to that category is akin to throwing it into a void within the void. After three months of sloppy cataloguing by Joe Public, 'Unknown' is clogged with items that somehow slipped into L-space from landfill, rotted beyond their original form. Cotton dresses with more holes than a colander, or toy robots with arms missing, filed alongside Thermoses and pepper shakers. That sort of thing. Not this sort of thing. Nothing genuinely new. He takes the screenshot to the unofficial *Florentine* message boards but everyone there is quick to call it another hoax, of which there have been many. Some members even trawl Declan's social media accounts to pull up information on his workplace to discredit him, as if the museum is about to become a curio showcase for Lost Space cryptids. Afraid the accusations might stir up trouble IRL, Declan asks the message board moderators to delete the messages and scrub his account. They do. He no longer exists in that world.

The only proof that he ever spotted the cephalopod in the first place is the screenshot sitting in his last message to Rob. It goes three days unseen. Four. Six. After a week of no contact—not even a read receipt—Declan closes the chat window. He calls in sick to work the next day. Nobody notices, they're overstaffed as it is. He has nothing left but the *Florentine*, its voyage through the dark, and the disposed, and the forgotten. Styrofoam mannequin. Catalogued. Butterfly collection. Catalogued. Georgian butter churn. Catalogued. Sleeveless vinyl record, Iranian jazz. Catalogued. A stone carved with a cross that must have meant something to someone, who knows how long ago. Catalogued. All in a jumble, a string of colourful handkerchiefs, a magician's wand and the carcass of a rabbit. Catalogued, catalogued—

Cephalopod.

In this photo, the tentacles curl towards or away from different areas of the lavender bubble, lit up green in bands of what looks like Morse code. If it is animatronic, it is unlike the other machines in Lost Space, still capable of movement. If it is an artwork it must be one of another unclaimed series, identical sculptures posed differently. But there's something in how the spacing of the cephalopod's suckers correspond to the puckered artworks, something in how the pearlescent eyes have locked onto the camera, that suggests this thing knows how to look, and how to be looked at. How to be seen. How to be alive.

This time, Declan keeps the discovery to himself. He doesn't archive it, or classify it, or try to place it in a box. He sits with it through the night, then makes himself a breakfast of stale cheese and crackers and eats in bed with his computer on his lap. He offers the cephalopod a bite by zooming in on the picture and holding the cracker up to its beak. It's meant to be a little joke, but it doesn't feel funny. There are too many tubes in the way of its beak for it to feed on anything. In a way, it looks like it might be on life support.

It dawns on him there are no others present in Lost Space. Not just other cephalopods, but no other life-forms, not even evidence of their existence. There are no rudimentary twigs lost by apes, no treasured shells abandoned by dolphins, no tribal idols carved by ephemeral beings who live on the moon of a distant gas giant. If Lost Space is a refuse site for the trash of an entire universe, it is full of the detritus of humans, and the artworks of the cephalopod, and nothing else.

Over the next few days, sightings of the cephalopod become commonplace. Declan sets up his computer, his tablet and his mobile phone so that each shows a different feed of photos of the alien as it tracks the human probe through Lost Space, always observing, never interacting. The *Florentine* Project message boards light up with theories and guesswork, as 'Unknown' becomes the most popular archive category. Holey cotton dresses might be death shrouds. Armless toys become pacifiers for babies with beaks. Fetish-wear with more straps than studs is re-contextualised as specialised garb for an inter-dimensional species, equipment to ensure survival in the absence of atmospheres and wildly fluctuating pressure.

how are you my love kiss kiss
sorry for zero chat, things have been wild
andre says hi! he can't wait to meet you, he's coming back with me
ugh what is that
didn't know you liked kalimari

First contact from Rob in four months appears as banners across all three screens, obscuring the cephalopod. Declan brushes them aside as if dusting something precious. When he peels himself from the crumb-strewn sheets, everything looks different. From framed posters on the wall to wedges of card under the television stand, from loofahs in the bathroom to nails holding down loose floorboards in the hallway, something is missing. He walks, barefoot and bleary-eyed, into the study. This was the first room they'd put together after moving in, even before the bedroom, because that's where they'd decided the bookshelves should go, and a house was not a home without books, or so Rob had said, although Declan had never thought of Rob as a keen reader, but the bookshelves were not now what caught his attention, but rather Declan's IKEA desk, which had lived several lives in several rental flats, broken down and re-made and reincarnated so often that putting it together had become a house-warming ritual. A desk which on this morning of clarity somehow looks flat-packed even when assembled. What little life the processed wood once held had suffocated in the void Rob had left behind.

Declan begins packing the very next day. All his books or fancy clothes go to a charity shop, as do Rob's, because while they look nice on the shelf or the hanger, that's all they seem to do. The framed artworks he auctions online, which more than makes up for the money he loses when he quits the heritage museum. As the spring weather dries up, he drags furniture through the house and into the street outside. If any of it had been antique he would have sold it, but it's mass-produced and disposable. Each time he leaves the house to get more cardboard boxes, another item has disappeared from the furniture pile, gone to a loving home, or into Lost Space to be inspected by the cephalopod, the handles and latches clumsy in its suckered tentacles.

Declan doesn't quite pare down the essentials to a set of feeding tubes, but he gets close. It takes a month to gut the house completely, but it feels like less. He knows he should mourn the connection he has with these objects, but he doesn't care. It isn't a loss; it's a relocation of matter. With a month's worth of supplies in a hiking rucksack, he stands on his doorstep and posts his keys back through the letterbox, along with a letter in a lavender envelope, his one concession to sentimentality. Everything that remains, he leaves to Rob and Andre. They can hold it in place until he comes back. That is, if he comes back at all.

As he opens the gate at the end of the garden path, light catches something small, green and glassy in the dirt.

LOVE IN THE AGE OF OPERATOR ERRORS

Shifting glass and neon typify the tech district of Edinburgh, sandstone traces of Leith subsumed by digital fascination, a transformation as startling and reviled as the New Town once was to the old city. These new builds respect the history of these streets, and hide their most innovative pleasures down lesser-known alleys. Somewhere in their shadows you hope you'll find Vincent. You followed his inexpertly-covered path to this strange fogged-window building tucked off the end of Leith Walk, its glassy heights reflecting the waterfront in dizzy blues and pinks. A sweep of buzzing light admits you. 'Welcome,' says a pre-recorded voice, 'to The Memory Jug. Share your story, renew your life.'

What the company's slogan lacks in substance, the foyer compensates for with ugly excess. Every surface, from the floors to the walls to the receptionist's desk, is overlaid with a clear resin, which gleams with embedded coins and pottery shards and loose rosary beads and glass eyes and a thousand more reminders that today's slick and smooth design was not always the epitome of beauty. There is little in the world still so deliberately messy as this. Vincent would have loved it.

After the split, your friends said they saw it coming from miles away. Polyamory was trouble and so was Vincent's desire that your relationship unfold into something the same but new, like a surprising origami. But other men made Vincent happy in ways you couldn't, and you wanted him to be happy. If he didn't disappear for a few days every so often, his energy would dim. He'd forget his house keys three days in a row, he'd forget to talk smutty in bed, he'd let the scrambled eggs cook dry in the pan even though you both liked them runny. When he strayed one morning and didn't come back, like a house cat gone away to die, all you had left of him was your jealousy, preserved like pennies under varnish.

The man behind the ugly reception desk greets you with disarming familiarity. You've done your research on the company so, if you had to guess, you'd place his accent as West African, with hints of old colonial French. Sure enough, when he hands you a clipboard, the name at the top of the attached liability waivers reads as Le Bijoux Mémoire.

'It's much prettier in French,' you say as you sign.

'We wait on more English forms from the printer,' he explains. 'The warnings are the same in either language.'

'You must be busy.'

'People enjoy to forget.'

You swallow hard against a lump in your throat.

'What if I wanted to remember something somebody else forgot?'

The receptionist clicks their tongue. 'People enjoy breaking rules.'

The Memory Jug specialises in reparative reality. People plug their experiences into its artificial intelligence, which behaves like a masseuse rubbing scarred tendons, psychological knots, over and over until they dissolve back into the body. A defrag for the mind at a reasonable price. Or so the brochure claims, but one man's reason is another man's lunacy. The email receipt for such services landed in your shared inbox like a grenade, and if you'd still been together, the four-figure cost of Vincent's last extravagance would have been reason enough to end it. Yet for some folk that's small change, and in return for cheap therapy the company holds records of everyone's trauma indefinitely. Useful when lobbying for more loopholes in data protection and planning permissions. Such a flexible culture, in such a precarious economy, makes for easy bribes. Your hands shake as you slide an envelope across the desk. Its contents: a copy of Vincent's account details and a pay-day loan you can't really afford. A glass eye stares up at you from the resin. The receptionist sweeps the envelope into a drawer.

'I want to see what he gave to you.'

Before long you're reclining on a well-worn leather couch in a white room, with a fish-bowl of sorts over your head, wires from the rim cascading down your chest to a tower of buttons. A woman in professional leisurewear flips and flicks switches on the side of a machine that appears to be nothing but switches. 'You understand this isn't what the technology is for?' she asks. She's West African too, and as she walks you through the process, you hear flecks of Edinburgh Morningside blended through her accent. 'There's no telling how individual consciousnesses interact with unfamiliar matter.'

'I was with Vincent for years,' you say. 'I'm not unfamiliar.'

She laughs. 'I'm just glad you signed the waiver.'

Wavelengths of Vincent's other loves begin to filter and rebound within the fish-bowl. As your reality slow-fades into his, a high pitched whine settles between your ears. A single spotlight at the subway tunnel entrance throws dancing shadows against a wall of corrugated iron, set across the tracks like a challenge. Broken bottles glitter in the grit between the sleepers and the rails, and the air vibrates with sound. When Vincent reaches up to wipe the sweat from his face you feel his hand upon your own brow. You are in his body, you share his mind.

The silhouetted crowd spits out Kevin the same way a cash machine dispenses hundred-pound notes: crisp, unhandled. His open-collared shirt and expensive shoes set him at odds to the other ravers, who sport dreadlocks and hoodies and sneakers. What are you, set against Kevin's bottomless wallet, but two out-turned pockets? Your gut sinks; you wonder if Vincent feels it, wherever he is. Instead, Vincent's heart quickens and you feel it in your own, a slippery sort of hope. Vincent is figuring out what of himself to share with this Kevin, what Kevin might have to give in return. This transaction hasn't been simple. It was Kevin's idea to come to the tunnel rave, but he stands by the entrance and watches the darkness jump. In the intermittent spotlight he looks around before taking Vincent's hand, to make sure it's safe.

An open relationship reshaped your boundaries. Vincent moved you from the edge to the centre of a puzzle you couldn't see until you'd already passed through it. With this overview you realise Kevin is a corner piece—or does that knowledge come from Vincent? Kevin's access to wealth is exciting and novel, but through Vincent you smell his complex aftershave, you taste the memory of expensive beer on his tongue, and you know Vincent hasn't yet told him about you or any of the others, because already, by the way he moves through the crowd, Vincent can tell that Kevin's not as generous with his love as he is with his money.

Dancing bodies part again and the spotlight sweeps across your vision, knocking you back into a leather chair. A skeleton staff presides over the Tristam's empty lobby of red leather and chrome. The barman idles by the piano, tripping up and down the scales with a sleep-deprived grace. This place is too far out of town, Vincent thinks, to be such a cliche. It's why no one stays here, why Audrey adores it; They can get as fucked as they like and they won't be asked to leave.

Because they're always here, buzzing like flies, occasionally they're asked to assist the night shift in their duties, as reparation for the taxis they never have enough money to pay for when dawn arrives. Tonight, they're helping change the bulbs in the chandelier. Audrey's strong hands hold the ropes tight, and she leans back to counterbalance the heavy ornament. The night concierge unscrews and re-screws and unscrews again, taking his time with the artisan coils, frayed and black inside glass domes. Audrey winks over her shoulder to Vincent. She's showing off. She's high. So is Vincent. The tectonic plates in his mind shift to convince himself he's in love, and not just in love with what Audrey supplies. The drugs are something Vincent doesn't share with you. The world is slow like treacle and you feel his quickbeat heart overlapping your own.

You hate this. The long mornings you had, the lazy afternoons and quiet day-trips to dune-banked beaches, you'd thought they were motionless moments in the chaos of living, lighthouses in the storm. Not burnouts and comedowns.

Where is your Vincent in all of this? *Your* Vincent. The possessive is embarrassing. Weren't the two of you beyond possession?

Vincent laughs, and you laugh with him, but you weren't paying enough attention to know where the joke came from. The night concierge gives a thumbs up, the barman flicks the switch. Let there be light. You watch Audrey's shoulders work under her wine-stained blouse as she and the concierge pull the chandelier higher, higher, higher. A communal halo hoisted back to heaven.

'Zip me up, sugar.'

Vincent's hands fumble with the zipper, which doesn't want to close across Margherita Slice's back. The vintage air hostess dress is a size too small for her and Vincent asks yet again why she hasn't asked one of her more experienced drag queen friends to alter it, so much more familiar are they with a sewing machine. Margherita uses her dressing room mirror as an intermediary to deliver Vincent a savage look, the sort you'd give a pet that doesn't know any better. Vincent enjoys the performance, lets the shade glance off him like mirrorball reflections. Margherita doesn't want to be convincing; and you hate how little effort she puts into everything, even Vincent, especially Vincent. You urge him to rip the tinfoil wig from Margherita's head, you want to ruin the half-hearted illusion and turn her back into Gerard, a risk analyst from Aberdeen. Vincent does no such thing. You're not in control.

Were he to sense this jealousy inside him, an alien presence, if he met you now for the first time—he'd turn away.

You root in his mind for the simulation's off-switch. The force of this desire warps the dressing room so that the ceiling bows and flexes upwards like a bubble. You hear a distant voice say something in French, but you don't understand. The drag show's compère welcomes Margherita Slice to the stage. She plants a fat and sticky kiss on Vincent's cheek, and as she pulls away you see pixellation around the corners of her eyes. She launches into her grim act: lip synching to black box recordings.

Christ, you hate her.

The entire midsection of Margherita Slice scrapes to the left in a rainbow glitch, digital innards spilling a cool white glow across the pillow of your bed. In the chill of a winter sunrise, the back of your own head is both impossible and familiar, like a cheap green-screen effect, or a photo of the dark side of the moon. Under the duvet, Vincent's left hand runs up your back and along your neck. You expect to feel his fingers on your body but you feel your body on his fingers. He tugs your earlobe. You remember that, from the last time you woke up together. A day later, he was gone.

Have these memories all been last encounters?

Then you—the remembered you—rolls to face Vincent.

Your entire face snags on some digital point, smearing a swatch of flesh tones across the orb of your skull. Your lagging face smiles, teeth showing through jaggy hair. One eye slides down onto the pillow in a puddle of pixels. You scream to be let out but Vincent's lips say, 'Hey, gorgeous.' He moves to kiss the glitching ogre.

And here's the thing: Vincent's heart beats slow.

The background whine, that tinnitus pitch, is gone. You thought it was part of the simulation, but it was within Vincent all along, until now. He is calm.

He is calm and you are the reason, and you're also the reason he's going to leave.

He's reached a conclusion you don't agree with: you are ambitious with your affection but you are not so good at sharing, and you deserve better, and he has to get away before he hurts you. He'll miss the others, but they won't care as much. If you'd known, if he'd told you, you would have said something to change his mind. He kisses you. You kiss yourself. If you'd known, you would have said something to change his mind. He kisses you. You kiss yourself. If you'd known, you would have said something to change his mind. He kisses you. You kiss yourself.

A disembodied voice breaks upon the scene: 'Monsieur, the feed is corrupting. We must take you back.'

Vincent rolls the lump of pixels that once was your body back over to the far end of the bed and falls asleep.

'The nearest exit may be behind you.'

Out of the darkness backwards walks Margherita Slice, leaving slivers of herself in the air. They twitch to the hollow beat of slow, reversed claps. When she spins to face you, her tinfoil wig and hostess costume remain facing forwards. Vincent has trouble unzipping her dress, the action feels unnatural.

'I bombed. Don't tell me otherwise. Air masks will drop from the overhead compartments. Too soon? Cabin prepare for landing.'

The dressing room projection bulges against the invisible fish-bowl. 'Non,' you hear the technician say. 'C'est coincé. Attendez qu'il soit chargé.'

The pause affords you time to study Margherita's expression. There is a secret smile under the scorn. Vincent is her guard dog. When she takes everything off and becomes Gerard, uncomfortable in her own skin, Vincent continues to call her by her name. You feel in Vincent the pride of protection. Despite everything, you feel pride too. You love that he cares enough to sustain the act. He is Margherita's standing ovation.

'Pan-pan, pan-pan,' says Margherita. 'Unsure of position.'

The Tristam's chandelier falls through the ceiling like a 747. Artisan light bulbs pull Audrey off her feet but, two inches into take-off, she lags. After five seconds stationary, she rises again by another foot. The upward movement presses her blouse down onto her shoulders. Another stutter upwards and the fabric rolls down her arms and chest like an oil painting given life. Suspended, Audrey winks, and winks, and winks. Vincent feels just as sluggish as the simulation. The lobby lights sting his eyes, his nose is running and his muscles ache. He took too much again, or mixed the wrong pills, a psychic exfoliation.

'You must hate me,' says Audrey. 'I'm always stringing you out.'

'No,' says Vincent, and you know it's true.

On rare occasions when your hangovers synchronised, or those weeks when you were both ill, passing the same bug back and forth, and the cost of being alive was a constant throbbing... Sometimes you loved Vincent most when you were nothing but two useless bodies holding each other together. That's what Vincent shares with Audrey: allowance and recovery, transaction and balance. But that's the limit of she got from him. You got the rest. He saved the best for you, uncut.

As Audrey's torso ascends to the ceiling her legs disconnect from her body and kick their way down into a sea of broken bottles. Kevin's knife-sleek car faces the tunnel mouth. Leaning against the driver door he reaches through the window and flicks the headlights into life. Vincent's shadow stretches out across the night's debris: crushed cans, discarded clothes, swathes of dead pixels.

'Even so, don't stop.'

'There's no music,' says Vincent.

Vincent dips his hips slow, raises his hands in the air. You have no choice but to be carried through the movements with him, each twist or thrust stirring bruised artefacts through the night air.

'Dance for me.'

'How do I apologise?' Vincent asks. 'For leading you on like this?'

Kevin floats backwards towards you, stray vectors rising off his body like steam. Vincent takes his hands and pulls him back into the rave, dancers coded out of darkness to press and grope under the railway arches. Kevin is looking for a love he can't buy, but Vincent isn't selling. He's afraid his generous heart might have a price, and he knows he can't afford to lose you. And now you know that, too. Vincent's smile, when it shows, spreads through you like a perfect fractal.

Blue screen.

White text.

erreur de système

rpc_s_invalide_liaison

métadonnée-incohérente

HEURISTIC_DOMMAGES_POSSIBLES

SXS_ROOT_DÉPENDANCE_MANIFESTE_NON_INSTALLÉ

avorter / refaire / échouer

It's dark when The Memory Jug kicks you out, but this innovative version of Leith doesn't need sleep. Neither do you, fired up by the experience, needing a connection. Neon arrows point you under awnings and into bars. You drink a whiskey alone, glad to taste something on your tongue that isn't someone else's beer. Around you, people stand close and drink and talk about deregulations in the digital sector. You don't understand a word. But a single glance down the length of a crowded bar can be an entire language in itself. An open relationship, you'd expected, would stretch you thin, make you love less, if more often. But as you were pulled back through Vincent's memories of loss, the opposite came to pass. You could love everyone in this aloof city if they let you. And you are open to it now, to the musical number at the end of the show where everyone, heroes and villains alike, get to be part of the chorus.

Will Vincent return to Le Bijou Mémoire? You hope so. That's the point of it. To go back, and back again, and drink of your hurt until the memory jug runs dry. But he's so hung-up on boundaries—moreso than you ever could have guessed—he might never get out of his own head.

Still, you have to trust he'll come back. It's the only way you have left of contacting him.

The technician had her doubts. Their machines, she explained, seek out neural pathways calibrated to sorrow, not joy, and anyhow, they don't have legal clearance to use this technology for pleasure. The risk of addiction is considerable.

But you appealed to their curiosity, and ountered that anyhow, they'd already broken so many laws, letting you inside Vincent's head, and they'd been familiar with the procedure, which suggests you're not the first to ask for the impossible.

If Vincent does return, there'll be a message waiting for him, wrapped up in a memory you've yet to create, an amalgamation of the good times, embedded in a new beginning that looks a lot like the first time you saw each other, in a bar not too unlike this one. There's no guarantee it'll work, but you have to pluck the dirty penny from the resin before you can see whose face is on the underside, and if the resin breaks, is that not beautiful, in its own way?

Renew our story, share our life.

MISCHIEF

Oliver liked to let the pit get filthy, but once again the Big Babies were on their way and they had high expectations.

Though required to start cleaning, he stood by Jungle World's exit and held his fidgeting hands behind his back, every bit the pliant servant. One last family was taking their time to leave the adventure playground, the mum cajoling both her five-year-old and her thirty-five-year-old into their jackets and shoes. Ridiculous, how long it took humans to become self-sufficient. Oliver fancied he personally had known how to tie his laces at age two. His own brood, meanwhile, were able to leave their mothers behind at three weeks.

In the wild some mothers can smell bad babies the second they fall out of their slits and they eat them up.

As if summoned by the thought, Nadia and Amy joined him by the reception desk. You only had to look at them to know they'd taken the Squid Slide down from the Jolly Rodger. Amy took a few seconds to re-adjust her uniform shorts, which had risen up into a wedgie, the fabric a lurid green that did nobody's thighs any favours, while Nadia's straightened hair stuck out from her head at all angles, charged with static. Neither seemed to mind how ridiculous they looked. What a curse to have so little self-awareness, so little pride.

Each girl had lied on her CV, their grander aspirations obscured for fear of seeming overqualified. A dirty trick for stupid people, unaware they were cheating themselves out of something better. Now that she was on the payroll, Nadia never missed an opportunity to remind everyone how these weekend shifts funded her undergrad degree in business psychology, and Amy was reluctant to join Oliver on a permanent contract, hoping to ascend into private childcare. Yet here they were, trapped with him in mediocrity. Oliver pitied their hope. Once you sank to his level of petty service, there was no getting out. After ten years of this shit, he knew.

Both girls were out of breath from running the Flush. A nightly ritual: two overlapping routes through the playground, designed to ferret out children who hadn't noticed the change in lighting, from fairytale pastel to warehouse white, nor the replacement of hyper pop with blessed silence. Often, these children had their reasons for being so oblivious to their surroundings. Not every kid had loving parents waiting for them in the cafe; not every kid with parents wanted them.

'How'd we do?' Nadia asked.

Oliver checked his watch. 'Five minutes, thirty-seven.'

'Nadia cheated,' said Amy. 'Saw her taking a short-cut round the bouncy castle.'

'You didn't have to tell him! Still, is that a record?'

'I've been faster.'

Oliver always told this lie to the new recruits, encouraging them to push their lithe young bodies harder and faster across the padded obstacle course. Sometimes they twisted their ankle in the safety netting, or concussed themselves against the low ceiling of a slide, and Oliver got to practice his concerned face. These two had yet to fall, but there was time enough for that tonight.

'Of course,' said Amy, 'You must've done the Flush hundreds of times.'

'Thousands,' said Oliver. 'Thousands.'

The slow parents waved goodbye with a queer wariness, as if seeing the Jungle World staff for the first time. Oliver smiled wider. His crow's feet and yellowed teeth added another five years to the decades already between himself and his colleagues. As the door shut behind the family, the father pulled his daughter in close and began to whisper to his wife. A warning, a decision not to come back. He imagined these parents watching tomorrow's news, holding their baby and saying, 'Oh my god, we were just there, that could have been us.' Oliver didn't mind. He knew he looked like the sort of man parents worried about, but their darling offspring had nothing to fear. Though they were disgusting and noisy and often intolerable creatures, Oliver had almost never wanted to hurt the children. It's what those children would become, which he despised.

Jungle World's after-hours events catered to grown adults celebrating promotions or graduations or stupid hipster weddings. In the privacy of his mind, Oliver called the participants Big Babies. Barging in half-cut from an expensive cocktail bar, still wearing office attire, the Big Babies enjoyed breaking the rules. Running where they shouldn't, throwing foam shapes, stopping themselves halfway down the chutes, or perversely even crawling up inside them. Anyone armed with even a smidge of pop-psychology knew what *that* was about.

Discipline, believed Oliver, was long overdue.

Yet for some reason the Big Babies never expected the place to smell of five hundred actual youngsters. Shitting, widdling, nose-bleeding babies. By the end of an average week there was no telling how much juvenile body fluid had spattered across the jigsaw blocks or dribbled down the free-fall slide. So while Nadia fetched the sprays and mops, and Amy began restocking the cafe, Oliver prepared to clean his pit.

He opened the back-room where they stored damaged furniture, broken toys, the parts of Jungle World that had succumbed to the ravages of children. In the corner was a busted-up playhouse. Hidden in the playhouse was a busted-up rucksack. The rucksack had kept him company from high school through to his medieval history PhD. And hidden in the rucksack was a secret Oliver couldn't wait to share with the Big Babies. He pushed open the playhouse's wonky pink door and looked upon the rucksack with fondness. It was the sort of bag a teenager would own. It seemed to be held together by badges, protest patches, and obscene scrawls of graffiti. Each adornment was a memory made by a version of himself Oliver no longer recognized. A punk, an activist, an academic on the rise. It was too laden with memories to throw away.

Inside, something picked at the stitches and scrabbled at the fabric.

Not yet, Oliver thought. *Be patient.*

The scratching stopped.

Obedient children.

It was dark here, and quiet; an urge to crawl into the playhouse stirred in Oliver's mind like oil on water, but with some concentration he resisted. There was work to be done. From the back of the warehouse he retrieved a large net scoop and six large rainbow tubs. He dragged them across the foyer to the lip of the ball pit. The fibreglass basin was set one and a half meters into Jungle World's floor, just deep enough to cause parental panic as children disappeared under its technicolor surface. In wide movements Oliver scooped the bright plastic balls into the tubs, and the pit's black base shivered into view. He unspooled a power hose to the pit's edge, and the jet of water rocked him back on his heels. He didn't believe the girls had the strength to control the flow, which was why he had hired them. Only he was allowed to clean his pit. He could hear Nadia and Amy moving around inside the play area but couldn't pinpoint their locations. He would have to sound them out before proceeding.

'How's it going?' he shouted over the noise of the hose.

'The usual.' Nadia's reply came from the haunted castle, where UV lighting showed every drop of the day's too-long-held piss, every splash of cake-and-ice-cream spew. 'What's the occasion again?'

'Some financial management firm,' Amy shouted from deep in the mushroom kingdom, a cage of rubber toadstools sprouting under a rope climbing frame. 'Can't remember the name, though.'

'Smith Whisenhunt Gray Advisory.' Confident neither of his colleagues could see him, Oliver cut off the flow, returned the hose to the damages warehouse and fetched his backpack. 'A research consultancy.'

'Dudes in love with the sound of their own names,' Amy said.

'A three-barrel name means a united front.' Nadia sounded peeved. 'Strength in numbers. It's prestige.'

Oliver laughed as he climbed down into the pit. 'They wouldn't call it prestige if it was worth anything. Who cares what your name is?'

But Oliver *did* care. After taking the booking for tonight's session, he'd hung up the phone in a daze. It couldn't be *that* Whisenhunt, could it? There weren't many Whisenhunts around. The thought was a constant irritant, a squeaky wheel in the corner of a darkened room, and with each turn Oliver felt the years settle on him like radioactive ash. It had been over a decade since they'd last seen each other, young-ish academics sharing a draughty office in the history department of a local university. Whisenhunt, a lazy sketch of a man, unkempt and fuzzy around the edges, had never known disappointment. He had slipped ahead of Oliver like a hagfish, slick and rank, coiling and coy, snatching awards and funding and laughing off his luck. The world tolerated such blithe humility for no good reason, as if being so shapeless, so nondescript, Whisenhunt had given the universe nothing to push back against. It was unfair, then, that the one thing he took a disliking to was Oliver's research. *Witches and trolls are for children,* he'd said often, *not historians.* So when it came to something true, something real and, yes, a little flawed, a mite unsavoury, of course the fool couldn't handle it.

But this time? Oliver was his own boss, and nobody was going to shut him down. Squirming backpack in hand, his noisy wheel of dark thoughts spun so fast, it felt like silence.

'Should we turn off the Slushee machine?' Nadia called from inside the haunted castle. 'You know, after last time.'

'Yes,' replied Oliver with urgency. None of them had ever seen vomit so *vivid.*

Down in the pit, Oliver listened to the drainage pipes gurgle. Even after a spray, the pit smelled ripe. Sweat, old socks, a tang of juvenile piss. There were territorial uses for urine in nature, of course, but Oliver didn't see the point if you were human, even a small human. To piss yourself was degenerate, no matter what size your bladder.

He crouched over the corner of the pit which he'd covered up with black duct tape. Layers and layers of the stuff. A tumorous mass covering a crack in the fibreglass, beyond which the foundations of Jungle World rattled with piping and AC ducts and the movement of small, sleek bodies. They moved in him, too: shivers of fear, dark shapes at the corners of vision, a hunger so constant, so very—

One of the girls shouted his name. He stuck his head above the pit's lip.

'Yes?'

'Sorry, Oliver. I didn't mean it!' Nadia sounded embarrassed.

'She said,' said Amy, 'she doesn't plan on mopping up baby poop all her life. And then she said, 'No offense, Oliver.''

'Ha ha,' he said. And then, to appear genuine: 'Ha ha ha.'

His squeaky wheel of thoughts flung sparks into the darkness.

Easy for you to think you're above this. Fucking stuck-up, purebred bitches. Give it ten years of sinking into shit. Climb the ladder fucking nowhere, for what? Blind motherfucking snakes, sucking at the tits of your own fucking egos mindless slugs go fuck yourselves leaving me behind I'll fucking—

He nearly shouted the violent thoughts into the play-park like an incantation, felt himself stiffen inside his lurid green shorts. This, too, he now shared with his brood. When they weren't thinking of eating or fighting, they were thinking of fucking. It brought his attention back to the crack in the ball pit's floor. A motionless furry snout poked through the clump of masking tape, the fur matted with adhesive. The desperation of the rat's attempt at escape from the playpark's underworld had bent back its long teeth, and a pink paw was jammed underneath the soaked snout, as if the rat had died while deep in thought rather than scrabbling for freedom. Oliver's hands shook as he cut the rodent free with the sharp edge of his house keys. Pinching the snout, he wiggled the animal forward, revealing the glassy black eyes, the comical ears, another little hand. And that was it. The entire back half of the rat's body was missing, the torso hollow of organs. A ragged flap of skin covered a gnawed ribcage. Oliver's hands stopped shaking, and his mind stopped sparking. He even allowed himself a smile. The occupants of this nest, he knew, were weak and wounded, pathetic, domesticated. For months he'd fed the mewling things table scraps in an effort to retain their trust, but if these sorry runts had resorted to cannibalism, that meant leftovers were no longer sufficient. He knew they were hungry. Now, they were angry, too. He could sense the desire emanating from them. No matter. A victory feast was en route.

Above him, the conversation had grown claws.

'I'm not saying there's anything wrong with having kids,' said Nadia. 'It's just not a milestone I *need* to reach.'

'And I'm not saying you *need* to reach it,' said Amy. 'I'm saying it's weird to shit on others for wanting to.'

'Parents should take some sort of test,' Oliver shouted up from the pit. 'Prove they know how to look after a living thing.'

'They already have that,' said Nadia. 'It's called a pet.'

'Pets are not trial babies!' said Amy. 'And what do you do if someone fails the test, sterilize them? That's inhumane!'

Oliver held his tongue. The girls weren't worth his time. He pried one corner of the duct tape free, then in several sharp rips pulled the whole mass from the floor. The crack in the fibreglass had grown from a slit the span of a child's hand to the size of a Jumbo Jungle Hotdog. Beond and through the crack, the smell of faeces and fur and damp was luxurious. Oliver stuffed the cannibalized rodent into his backpack's side pouch, then removed from the main compartment something large and soft, wrapped in a bloodstained towel.

His Rat King.

The beast was supposedly mythical, a group of rodents so unclean their tails had stuck together, a tangled family that lived and died as one being. Some long-dead scholars believed that to find such a sinister omen would grant the lucky discoverer dark forces of control. From yellowed tomes kept in glass cases, to old wives' tales scratched in the margins of cookbooks and almanacs, the folklore said he was supposed to have stumbled across the thing by accident. Oliver often imagined the Bubonic Plague hadn't been an accident, but payback, proof that a clever individual such as himself could rise to power on the crest of a black wave. Total control over little scared things was not to be underestimated.

But Oliver was too old to rely on happenstance. He couldn't waste time roaming woodlands, *hoping* to trip over a Rat King. So he took matters into his own hands. His first attempt to hurry things along, undertaken during his postgraduate degree, had been a filthy cage overstuffed with rodents, hidden in the history department's disused boiler room. An effort to encourage organic entanglement. In truth, all it encouraged was an aroma that wafted through the department's ventilation system. Oliver had enjoyed the stench of ammonia, nothing more than a symptom of the first stage of the project. He had filled his lungs with it, daydreaming of Winona and Susie and Jasmine and all the others packed tight and snug.

Whisenhunt was not so enamoured with the smell and roamed the building, gagging and demented, until he found the cage in the boiler room. The old clunker of a furnace hadn't been used in years but Whisenhunt fired it up and flung the rats in one by one, as if sensing the dark potential of the nest, until the basement's aroma changed from furry fear to bad barbecue.

In retrospect, Oliver shouldn't have given the rats individual names.

He was asked to take some time off and never asked to take it on again. Meanwhile, Whisenhunt, the mass murderer, sailed on to greater things with a whistle and a song. Fucking typical.

But tonight, fate tipped its hat to Oliver. What luck! And this new Rat King was much better than the first. Catching the rats had been the simplest thing. Components found on site: crepe paper sheets spread with cheap jam, laid over empty five-gallon paint buckets, their insides slathered with Vaseline from the first aid kit. He'd positioned the traps behind Jungle World's recycling bins, listened from his office as they filled with a thud and a squeak, a thud and a squeak, a thud and a squeal and a squeak. He'd picked out the fattest, strongest rats. They were to be his princes. The runts, meanwhile, he returned to Jungle World, through the fissure in the fibreglass. Underneath the building was as good a place as any, for them to run free and shit and fuck. Especially to fuck. There must be six dozen or so by now, Oliver reckoned. A sizable family. Survival of the fittest hinged not on brute strength but numbers, and tonight, Oliver was going to win.

Getting the chosen ones home had been a hassle. Training them? A joy. If he was to exert control over all other rats they'd ever sired, and their young, and *their* young, it stood to reason that the King also must be fit to fight at his command. His bathtub became an arena for pitched battles. But though he'd picked the biggest and the best, conflict wasn't in their nature. They soon settled into a ratty hierarchy, and refused to fight anyone but him. So he introduced wild-cards: drugged stray cats, pigeons with their wings pinned back. If the brutal scuffles got him stiff, which they often did, he masturbated into the bloody tub, and the victors licked from the enamel his raspberry-rippled semen. When the time came to tie his battle-scarred babies together, folding the pink-white tails around each other, feeling the bones inside crack and splinter, the rats were so scared of him, they didn't even try to bite. As he super-glued shut the last loop of warm skin he saw their black eyes shimmer like oil on water. The thing turned its heads towards him as if mesmerized, one mind under his control, and he felt something inside *him* tighten and flex with new strength, too.

Now, down in the stinking pit, the Rat King stirred and pawed at the air as Oliver folded it into the crack in the floor, taking care to protect its scars, some still weeping pus. If the scrolls and parchments were to be believed, proximity to the Rat King's own kind would deepen the connection between Oliver and the runts he'd left to breed in the hidden hollows of the play-park. The darkness squeaked at him, a pledge of allegiance. This time, he did not seal up the crack in the fiberglass floor. His babies were free to roam, to explore, to play. With the rat king as a conduit, he would call the leftover runts into the light for a parade of sorry heroes. A graduation, of sorts.

'Have you kissed and made up?' he called into the playground.

'We weren't arguing,' Nadia said.

'Yes, you were,' Amy shot back.

Beanbag Room. The Playhouse. No witnesses.

He hauled himself out of the pit, and filled it with six new tubs of clean plastic balls. The rainbow colours stacked up and up, settling and shifting. With the long arm of the net he smoothed the surface until it was uniform and flat. He stored the apparatus then strolled along Flush Route One, squirting air freshener to make it smell nice for the delicate, squeamish, soft-minded Big Babies.

For the first time in a decade, he felt prepared to face the future.

Yet Whisenhunt's arrival came as a shock. The man half-burst, half-stumbled through the entrance doors, trailed by an entourage of forty guests, and it seemed to Oliver as if the primary colours of Jungle World brightened into neons. A decade of success had transformed Whisenhunt, his shaggy haircut now buzzed tight, his pasty researcher's skin almost golden, shiny grey suit tailored to an effortful body. His old swagger and charm had gone nowhere, but seemed to have hardened from a vague aura into an invisible armour. As Whisenhunt approached the reception desk, Oliver felt an itching in his mind, a low panic. He shut his eyes and calmed his thoughts. Whisenhunt clicked his fingers in Oliver's face. Oliver yearned to bite them clean off.

'Alright, mate?' Whisenhunt said. 'We're here for the, you know, what's-it-called. Mature fun. The name's—'

'I know who you are.'

Oliver paused, to allow Whisenhunt a chance to recognise him, to understand who he was talking to. But the moment passed. Instead, Whisenhunt made a show of writing a check, performing the largesse of management, and laid it on the counter under Oliver's open hand. He expected Oliver to lift it like a candy wrapper. Oliver stared at him in silence. Whisenhunt relinquished, and slapped the cheque into Oliver's palm. A petty victory, not what Oliver desired. He stared a little longer, hoping he might see shame or fear creep across Whisenhunt's taut face.

'What? Not enough? You want a tip?'

'No sir,' Oliver heard himself mumble. 'That's everything, thank you, enjoy your evening.'

How could Whisenhunt have forgotten him? He slunk away to the cash office. A decade must have rendered him as unrecognisable to Whisenhunt as Whisenhunt now was to him. But where Whisenhunt had grown, Oliver had bloated. Where Whisenhunt had bloomed, Oliver had wilted. Hunched and pinched, fatter and hairier, twitchier with shiny anxious eyes. As if year by year a little more of him had been eaten away by invasive black mold. What was the point of revenge if the victim didn't recognize his revenger?

It was Nadia's turn to deliver the safety spiel: emergency exits, medical information, no stopping halfway down the slides. Of course, none of the Big Babies listened. They swarmed the playground, women running ahead while the men tried to play it cool, sauntering over to the cafe and rolling their eyes, as if they'd been coerced into this. He pretended not to notice the flasks of whisky and vodka the Babies tipped into their overpriced coffees and juices. *Let them have their fun,* Oliver thought, *before I have mine.*

The same night he constructed the Rat King, he'd tested the thing's powers. *Come to me,* he'd commanded. Experts said you were never more than several feet from a rat, as if there was going to be just one. There was never just one. Rodents spilled from cracks in his bedroom walls, thrust their way through light fixtures in the ceiling, burbled up the U-bend in his toilet. Screams and panic filled the flats above and below as he conjured vermin from the shadows. Oliver had sensed their consciousness scrabbling inside his head, the beating of their tiny hearts inside his chest. He selected several minds from the mass and bid them to sit in formation on his kitchen table. They did, they really did. An instant hunger boiled up in him; it was all they thought about, if they could be said to think at all. Under that impulse he felt their meekness in his mind as if it were his own, and twitched with inherited fear, but steeled himself to rise above it. They could rise above it too. The Rat King would funnel Oliver's anger into each of his bewhiskered subjects until they filled up with bloodlust, and allowed his force of will to overcome their nervy, twitchy instincts.

Rough hoots shocked Oliver from this sweet reverie. He turned his attention to the men swinging from the monkey bars. It was some sort of competition. One of them was Whisenhunt, who had wrapped his big thighs around a competitor's waist and was thrusting his hips up into the man's face, complete with performative grunting. Oliver marvelled at how such a dull brute could have survived academia. The absolute child, the fucking imbecile. Greased palms, sliming through the world's grip. He deserved what was coming to him. Every single one of them deserved it. Payback for their hollow successes while clever, decent people—people like Oliver, who'd never had the same chances—were forced to simper like inbred lapdogs.

Nadia offered Oliver an espresso someone had ordered then refused. 'You good, boss?'

'Worried about my kids,' he said.

'Didn't know you had any.'

'They're right here.' He massaged his temples. 'They're all right here,'

He drank the coffee. The caffeine should have helped him concentrate, but it amplified his agitation. With all his preparation, he hadn't expected that he wouldn't be calm, but he was not calm. He heard raised voices, and flinched. Amy was waving her arms at someone, shouting something. Oliver had to force himself out onto the floor. Everything was too loud, and too bright.

At the back of the ball pit, Whisenhunt had scrambled several meters up the metal cage wall, thick fingers straining at the mesh.

'Excuse me! Excuse me sir! Sir!' Oliver wanted to call Whisenhunt by his name, but kept defaulting to the trained politeness of subservience. He didn't understand how Whisenhunt didn't know who he was. 'You are not allowed to climb on the equipment like that!'

'Fuck off, we paid for this!' Cheers burst from Whisenhunt's co-workers in the pit. Others deeper in the Jungle emerged to watch.

'You are breaking the rules.' Oliver's voice came out shrill. His connection to the Rat King brought interference. The smell of the place below, layers of damp, hot bodies, stuffed up his head like an inflated balloon. A panic too large—too many of them sharing his mind. They'd bred too much, too fast. 'There will be a penalty!'

'A penalty, aye?' Sinew and muscle shifted under Whisenhunt's shirt as he pulled himself farther up. 'Gonna make me wear that ugly uniform? You look like a paedo!'

Oliver felt Amy's hand on his arm, heard her say something about refusing to reward bad behaviour. Nadia was there too, advising de-escalation, conflict management. But Oliver didn't want to de-escalate anything. He wanted the man in the suit in the pit with the rats in his head with the rats in his head the rats in his head in his head in his head.

He took a deep breath.

'I'm warning you,' he said. 'Get down.'

The nest was quiet. All stood up on hind legs, sniffing the air for danger. This time, Oliver *was* the danger, full to the brim with thoughts of tanned limbs bitten raw and bloody. He was ready to overflow, ready to show them all. Just as soon as Whisenhunt saw it was him, as soon as Whisenhunt knew his place and said he was sorry—or said that he wasn't, any trigger would do. Whisenhunt had to understand, his position had shifted, from greasy prince to underdog, so that when the rats came for him, when they swarmed up his body like a black tide, he would know he'd been wrong, so wrong, to underestimate Oliver's potential, back then, and now, and forever.

Whisenhunt cocked his head to the side, took in Oliver's squared shoulders, his fierce glare, his warrior stance.

This was it.

Recognition.

'Get a life, jobsworth.'

The nest scattered.

'I had a life!' Oliver screamed. 'You ruined it! You... you...'

His tongue flicked around inside his mouth, searching for an ancient curse that might set Whisenhunt's head aflame, cause his heart to rot inside his chest, flick his skin into the air like a soiled wet wipe.

And yet.

'You Big Baby!'

All those years studying the arcane, wasted in this moment.

'Who're you calling baby?' Whisenhunt swung carefree from the mesh, mugging faux offence for his entourage, who fell into fits of laughter. 'Nah, mate, nah. You've got me confused with someone else.'

Oliver quivered. The nerve to come here, *right here*, into Oliver's shitty work, to flaunt success, to lie, and humiliate, and refuse to play the game? No, that would not do at all. That was not part of the plan.

'You're not gonna chuck us out, are you, jobsworth?'

'On the contrary,' said Oliver. He located the Rat King in his mind. He'd worked too hard not to see that man scream for mercy. Everything was in place, everything was perfect except for that spark of recognition. But he didn't need it, he'd never needed it, he could do this for himself, and for himself only. He felt a sickly smile spill across his face. 'I'm going to make sure none of you ever—'

'Cannonball!'

Whisenhunt let go of the cage, and fell into the pit. Plastic balls rose into the air like shrapnel. The impact shook Oliver's mind, he heard it with his whole being, with a hundred others, tiny hearts thudding too fast to count the beats. Oliver hoped to see a twitching nose, a long tail threading through the plastic.

Rise up, he thought through the panic.

Nothing.

Oliver felt squeezed and spineless like something trapped

underwater. That multitudinous strength, tightened by his connection to the King, had slipped loose.

Rise up, he pleaded in his mind. *Avenge me!*

But his anger had been diluted.

A drop of blood in a lake of meek, mild milk.

Whisenhunt sat upright in the pit, plastic balls rolling in to pack the space around his chest. 'Let me speak to your manager,' he said. He looked impossibly young, younger than Oliver remembered. The gilded life hadn't just rewarded Whisenhunt, it had rejuvenated him. Success, its own kind of magic. 'Let me speak to someone in charge, or else I'll throw a tantrum. Like a baby. Like a big, smelly baby!' He had the gall to wink before falling backwards, pounding on the fibreglass, kicking balls into the air, red, blue, green.

A barrage of sonic booms brought Oliver to his knees. Amy hooked her arms under his armpits and helped steer him to the staffroom. He saw darkness where there was none. He felt wetness on his thighs. Amy dabbed at his crotch with a towel, then paused, disgusted, pushed the damp towel into his hand. Words were spoken which he only half-heard. Grown man. Take care. Then she left him, shivering and sobbing, alone.

The Rat King was in his head, knotted, clawing at itself. Too aware of its own creation, no longer a conduit under his control. But the connection persisted, the flow reversed; he clogged up with natures not his own, like a pipe too narrow to cope with the filth it had to ferry. He forced himself out of the cheap plastic chair but at the staffroom door the multitude inside him revolted and he scurried back under the lunch table. He fought the urge to lick himself for comfort, afraid the hunger he felt in a stomach that wasn't his own would turn the comfort into compulsion, and he'd bite, he'd bite, he'd bite.

Nadia checked in on her way out. With none of Amy's maternal instinct, she let him know they'd run the Flush to clear out the drunks and shut down the cafe. He asked her to call an ambulance but it came out in hiccupy squeaks and squeals. 'Whatever the fuck is up with you,' she said, 'it's above my pay grade.'

Visions of spring-loaded traps and poisonous pellets moved in him like shadows along the edges of a room, afraid to be thought. He imagined bringing a hammer down on the Rat King's heads and felt the blow on his own skull.

He heard doors slam, the rumble of cars leaving the car park. Jungle World was quiet now. Oliver crept out onto the floor, twitching at each creak and groan as the building cooled down. He flinched at his own grumbling stomach. Nadia had switched off the lights, yet he could see just fine. The bright primary colours frightened him. Astounded at the acuity of his senses, he followed a food smell up into the mushroom kingdom, where a half-eaten hotdog lay on the floor. He held it to his mouth but felt guilty. This wasn't his hunger. This wasn't his hotdog.

Invisible hands took hold of his limbs and turned him around, filled him up with compliance. As he approached the pit, its surface became animated. Flicks of tails and claws under the rainbow spheres. Lumps of charcoal with bubblegum mouths. He threw the hotdog into the pit. Unseen paws pulled it under the surface, and he tasted stale bread, bad mustard. It wasn't enough. The hunger of a hundred tiny stomachs.

His brood, his plague, his mischief. Waiting for him. Patient babies. They called to him. Pushed him forwards. Made him obey.

Oliver lowered himself into the pit.

Warm black bodies swarmed up his shirt, down his shorts, over his throat and head. Tiny things, shivering with excitement. They nipped and bit and peeled back his flesh. Their broken tails flicked through his hair. Their tiny hands opened up his chest.

Oliver let them in. He let them all in.

THE
NAPLES SOLDIER

At the church doors a sleep-eyed girl blocks my path. I try to remember her name. Mary or Edith, something short and unusual. Everything is still strange, especially remembering, especially names. My anxiety stabilisers, my remote memory, every other useful part of me lies bloody and useless on a surgeon's table five hundred years in the future. Shame the same can't be said for my accidental companion. I tell Mary-or-Edith why I'm here. The girl's eyes narrow, but she lets me in, and waves an open palm at the rows of bunks which have replaced church pews. Three strands of guilt bloom and intertwine in me like razor wire: survivor, observer, perpetrator. Some of the bunks' occupants cough terribly, some moan and writhe. Some who do neither are asleep, and some are dead.

Halfway down the hall, Dr Mandel looks up from a dozing patient, his mouth and nose protected by nothing more than a white cotton face mask. A crude precaution. He nods at me, but is in no hurry to speak to me. In this pandemic, one sick person is as sick as the next.

But my sick person is *special*. Archie Findlay: art collector, skilful propagandist, hopeless bigot. My only friend. Despite everything he is, everything he might become, I am here to protect him, and without medical attention, he will die. Perhaps he may still die. Stripped of my data filters, my probability index, I am uncertain of everything. What am I meant to do, if Archie's illness uploads him to the great beyond?

It took six months to find someone so well-connected, so weak-willed. A further six to stoke his baffling hate to a fever pitch. I expect another six months will pass before he'll leave Glasgow for Munich or Dresden, under my guidance, to join the Nazi party. Not that such a party exists yet—but it will. Archie must put himself forward as an expert on fine art restoration and curation, all the better to help the party reshape Europe in their own image. With my help, he will eventually find himself in the same room as history's second-greatest butcher.

First place, of course, now belongs to me.

Dr Mandel steps away from his patient and ambles towards me. He's much shorter than the average man of this era—his standard-length white coat breezes about his ankles, and he is eye-level with my bellybutton. He does not look up at me. He knows why I'm here, and is reluctant. For someone like Archie, this doctor would sway the Hippocratic oath, and I don't blame him. With his medical black clutch in hand, Mandel follows me to Archie's tenement flat. On the way there I wonder, not for the first time since arriving in Glasgow, whether or not I should kill myself.

It would be easier to do so now than any time before. Easier for me, too, than for any of those who I trained with. I've watched as comrades, broken and brave, the business end of a pulse rifle held under their chin, begin to laugh. Their vitality chip overclocks. Their brains flood with dopamine, serotonin, oxytocin. They feel at ease for just long enough to remember to live, even if they don't want to. No happy-juice for me, here in the twentieth century, era-incongruous enhancements ripped clean from my body in preparation for my mission. No longer held in place by a vitality chip, I should be able to fling myself from the peak of Arthur's Seat and be done with it. An organic death. A romantic notion.

Come the autopsy, though, what would these primitive doctors make of my innards? That maze of bionic tubes threaded through my guts? They might mistake me for a German spy, or a demon, or both; superstition has yet to leave this world. More likely they'll trigger a blast right there in the morgue and turn to shadows in an instant. I am the pulse to my own rifle. A deadly payload not meant for them.

The assassination of Hitler. Late second millennial fiction was rotten with the idea, the regret of poor decisions hanging over the world like an unshakable malaise. By the start of the third millennium even the most talentless storytellers found the idea hackneyed, deployed only as entertainment. Several near misses later, at the weary remove of five hundred years, the people of the twenty-fifth century could barely remember the war, let alone care. It didn't matter whose side had lost more lives, which armies surrendered, which cities were flayed from the map. It was merely a story, a once upon a time, and the dead existed only as statistics. With the discovery of time displacement, however, history condensed into a single immediate now, and those numbers became incomprehensible.

A horror, to our modern minds, that so many should even be alive to die, but was it not our responsibility to do something, anything, if we could? There were disagreements of how, exactly, we should proceed, and fears of alternate timelines, temporal loops, the theorised elasticity of causality... The disagreements were, quite literally, inconsequential. Whether we changed history or not, it made no moral sense not to *try*.

In an ideal universe I would have beamed into Hitler's nursery and ended it there, a pillow held over the babe's screaming face, but the displacement process is less precise than that. The world moves through space as well as time, and I am lucky not to have materialised on the moon, or in the forests of Pangea. As things stand, I'll have to make the best of Scotland, 1918. But once I gain access to the Führer's inner circle I will break my own arm. The rush of endorphins will trigger a gut reaction. I will explode, and prevent the second world war of the twentieth century. In doing so, I'm meant to save seventy million lives.

Yet before the war even has a chance to begin I will have killed one hundred million more.

Archie's tenement flat is cold enough to mist our breath but you wouldn't know to look at him, stripped naked and feverish atop his bedsheets. Businesslike, Dr Mandel snaps open his clutch, removes a thermometer, waves it like a magic wand to reset the mercury. He clutches Archie's jaw a little too tightly and jams the thermometer under Archie's tongue. This seems crude to me. I suppose come the fourth millennium, doctors will look back on treatments I've endured, and find them just as reckless, if not moreso.

'I've seen worse.' Mandel prescribes two aspirin every hour until dawn. I don't want to doubt his expertise but this seems too much. My right hand flits to my temple, expecting a sub-dermal switch that facilitates access to military medical databases from here to Alpha

Centauri. There is only a scar. Two years ago I was the walking embodiment of military innovation; tonight, I'm no wiser than the corpses crowding trenches at the Somme.

I show the doctor out, but at the door he turns and says, 'You're not like him, are you?' I shake my head: seven foot tall, scarred all over, I'm not like anyone else on the planet. He continues: 'He is not your responsibility. You might think different, perhaps you fought together and you feel… a brotherhood? But as to why you might…'

He's unsure of how far he can push the topic without provoking me, but then his eyes flare bright he steps back to make eye contact.

'If you were in his place, Archie would not come to me for help.'

I thank Mandel and let him go back to his clergy of needy patients. In the bedroom Archie moans for a glass of water, then coughs up so much phlegm it dribbles from the corner of his mouth. I fetch a cloth and wipe away the muck. I carry the cloth to the bathroom to wash it clean. What does Dr Mandel know of responsibility? At most he is custodian of a mere couple hundred lives. In the murky gaslamp light my gaze flits between the phlegm on the cloth and my sliced-up face in the mirror, as if the connection between my body and the greenish-white mass might hold some sort of answer.

I try to sleep. Though the memory of my journey is clouded and difficult to grasp while I am awake, it returns to me in dreams of perfect clarity.

The temporal displacement facility is a patchwork miracle orbiting Titan, the teleportation compartment a mess of wires and screens. I stand on a central raised platform, naked. A hologram of my supervisor flickers into view. She lets me know systems are fine, that this should be a breeze. I feel a tingle in my skull, just behind the eyes. I don't think to say anything.

A gravitational current shocks me three feet into the air and holds me there. It stretches my arms outwards, the fresh scars along my wrists glowing blue with electricity and time, unbound. The time cube pops into existence around me. Through its walls I see a field of corn, in the distance an airfield launching biplanes into a rainy sky. Men run from a barracks to a hangar. They are soldiers too, but there is as much in common between us, as there is between their aeroplanes and a wooden trebuchet.

The head-tingle intensifies, and I sneeze.

Concern in the control room, then panic. Red lights flash rhythmically like a heartbeat, a siren sounds, but it is too late to reverse the process. I feel corn stalks brushing my bare thighs, I smell the soil under my feet, I hear the roar of propellers tearing up the sky.

I am an agent of biological warfare. My body is a living explosive. But too late, we realise I am not the only organism travelling back in time armed with five hundred years of history, five hundred years of progress.

Survivor, observer, perpetrator. Trojan horse. You'd think this pandemic, which in a single year will set humanity back to the sum of one hundred million, would have left a scar more memorable than any war, but we did not know, we did not know.

Archie wakes me with a coughing fit. I take a glass of water to him. 'Good man,' he says between sips and aspirin, causing the barbed-wire guilt to constrict tighter in my chest. 'Good man.'

He could have been a good man too, before I curdled his spirit with fearmongering and hate. I hope when I detonate he is standing somewhere behind me, so I don't have to look at his face, don't have to watch him bear that last split-second of betrayal. And as much as I think I deserve it, I cannot kill myself before then. If I do, then his death, and these hundred million others, will have been in vain.

Yet I have hope. Though I'm no historian, though I come from so far away, I cannot recall any common knowledge of this carnage. Surely we do not forget our collective past so swiftly, so completely? There was no record of it in our archives. Perhaps there will be, now.

I have changed history already, that much is clear and terrible. But if history can be changed, I must stay the course.

There are miseries ahead which must never be remembered.

DEAD SKIN

The Giantess serves no purpose. Ten foot tall, skin painted yellow, she pushes her daffodil breasts up between her outstretched arms. Objections have been filed against her. She's an ornamental remnant of the building's tawdry past, once a strip club, now a gym. On the wall beneath her, the squat rack's mirror reflects my own impossible body, huge and sculpted. Nobody complains about me. The steel bar across my shoulders so loaded with weight, it groans. Polyblends strain against my curves and dimples. I tense this body, feel it fill with power, and grunt to rise, stand tall, impossible, indominitable, unapproachab—

'Can I work in?'

It's poor etiquette—dangerous, even—to butt in like that, but I rack the bar and turn to see who's asking. Round-faced and ginger-haired, their soft body shows the first sign of hardness and bulk. A green pin badge on their t-shirt bears their pronouns: *ne/ nir/ nem*. They seem new enough to merit a pass.

'How heavy do you want it?' I ask.

Nir eyes flick to the bar, whites showing all the way around. I remove plates from the bar until it is empty, and ne nods. As I step out from the rack, nir gaze settles on the scar that weaves a ring around my throat, and I let nem stare. My two skins contrast: white-pink from the neck up, freckled tan all the way down. The medical term for the operation is cephalosomatic anastomosis; a head transplant. I am easy to look at in the same way mermaids and three-legged men are easy to look at.

I clear my throat, Adam's apple bouncing on the scar like a tightrope walker. 'What're you training for?'

'I'm a stage-hand.' Ne points to the image on nir T-shirt, a pair of gurning masks, the logo of a nearby theatre. 'Lots of picking things up and putting them down again. I'm so out of shape. Used to be fitter, but I... had to take a break.'

'Over-training?'

'Something like that.' A flinching smile. 'I'm Gale, by the way.' Ne offers a clumsy handshake.

'Bruce.'

'The Modern Frankenstein,' ne says. Of course ne already knows who I am. *Everyone* knows who I am. The documentaries, the controversies, the clickbait. I'm an urban legend in my own lifetime, a meat-head monster and medical miracle. If Gale notices my discomfort with the nickname, ne doesn't show it. Ne gets into position in the rack. Ne's attentive to form—'Is my stance wide enough? How's my posture? Where do I put my hands?'—but soon loses balance. I'm there to catch nem, providing support in all the right places.

Gale smiles, leans into me. 'It's been a while since anyone tried to pick me up.'

So *that's* nir game. Gale's attraction sends a surge of emotion up through my chest, and deeper down, capillaries opening all in a rush—but the sensation stops short at my scar. Some slap-dash surgical error robbed me, among other things, of a blush reflex.

For every ninety-nine who look at this body with disgust or fear or incomprehension, there's one who gets off on it; who wants to be lifted, and intimidated. Who can blame them? On days when I'm a stranger to myself, I try to approach this body of mine the same way others do, unsure whether to tremble in pleasure, or fear. I look up at the Giantess, half-expecting her to laugh at my soft interior, but she's as stone-faced and useless as ever.

Here, if nowhere else, I'm aspirational.

Lit by neon signage, Sally breathes mist into the night, pretending not to see the group of men swaying in front of us, pretending sobriety. She hates these shifts running security for Pink Salt; the venue insists on gender-balanced security, but would change their tune if they ever heard her staffroom banter. When she works the door for Pink Salt, she won't talk to anyone if she can help it, so annoyed is she by the clientele. She leaves it to me, to ask the question:

'You know what kind of night this is?'

The young men stammer yes, they know what kind of night this is. A tipsy riot of piercings, odd haircuts, secret bodies under shapeless coats. I step aside. They descend the stairs to the basement bar. They'll fit right in.

The door below slams shut.

'How long till the body's yours?'

The bouncer job is easy and the high-collared uniform hides my scar, but ever since our first shift together, Sally's been nothing but questions. There's no denying the fact of my body, of course, but I'm prohibited from naming the scientists and doctors who gifted it to me. When documentaries are made about the miracle of me, my creators get to hide behind mirrored glass, or sit in darkened rooms with their voices altered. Their generous military benefactors are similarly cloaked in legalese. Much like the identity of tonight's clubbers, Sally takes the ambiguity of my origins as a personal affront. What I first mistook for empathy has revealed itself as a sort of cruel interrogation, more interested in poking wounds than letting them heal. And they *have* healed: I finished the bespoke cocktail of hormones and drugs as of last month. I don't tell Sally this, though; she gets off enough on my progress as it is, there's no need to encourage it.

'I'm just saying,' she continues. 'There's more of it than there is of you. You're the... er, foreign object.'

She huffs into her hands and rubs them together for warmth. My silence annoys her.

'Whatever, man,' she says. 'Your life, your choices.'

'It's not like I had other options.'

'Aye, you did.'

'It was this or a casket.'

Sally looks like she has something more to say, but shuts up when another battalion of androgynes rounds the corner and sings towards us.

'Bru-ucie! Big Brucie boy!'

A familiar laugh rises steep like an alpine climb. I force myself to remember my uniform, my function. What use is a shield that can't take a few blows? The crowd parts and a queen limps to the front. Despite everything, she looks well.

'Hello, Glenda,' I sigh. 'Long time, no see.'

'Oh, I wouldn't say that,' she says. 'I see you everywhere, all the time. You made the news. We were all so proud of you.' She simpers close. I can see the glue along her lacefront, smell the grease of her lipstick, her pupils dilated so wide there's almost no iris. She's on more meds than I ever was, just to stand upright unassisted. 'I mean, just look at you. Rough and tough and strong and mean! What a prize.' She hovers a hand over my crotch. Her voice drops an octave. 'Shame the body ain't yours to have.'

Sally stands a little taller. 'Bruce?'

'It's nothing,' I say. But it's not nothing. I can't remember the last time I broke a sweat through fear of being seen for who I am. Not even in my old body; people either saw my illness before they saw me, or didn't see me at all. Under examination I chafe against my own skin from the inside, a snake unable to moult.

'Don't call me nothing, big man.' Glenda bristles. 'Weren't for me, you'd still be a crip like the rest of us.'

'Go on in, ladies,' I say, heart pounding. 'Please.'

Descending to the basement, Glenda leads the group in song: 'Cause you make me feel! You make me feel! You make me feel like a natural—' The basement door slams shut on her voice.

Sally, quite predictably, demands an explanation.

'We were in the same pool of applicants,' I say. 'Glenda referred me. For treatment.'

Sally snorts. 'Bet she's not called Glenda in the morning.'

It's the second-to-last thing Sally says to me all night. I no longer fit so neatly into her idea of me. At first glance, this body is too brutish to be anything but what she expected, I'm not meant to be one of the unclassifiable ones, I'm not meant to know drag queens by name. It's not my fault she thinks I tricked her. She tricked herself.

But her car-crash curiosity re-emerges to poke at one last wound:

'What did he mean, not yours to have?'

*

When we first met, now shy of a month ago, Gale had been quick to roll nir eyes at men grunting as they benched, thinking it all too performative. Every time powerlifters dropped their hundred kilo burdens to the mats, ne'd flinch at the noise, the shake of the floor. Today, however, in position beneath the Giantess, Gale slings weight onto the barbell with new confidence, more than I expect nem to be able to lift. I reach over to place one big hand on nir chest, the other at the base of nir spine, and with a little pressure I straighten nir stance. Gale's breathing changes. A red-faced grimace of effort camouflages any blush or smile. I count nem down from ten, reminding nem to exhale and stand tall, but ne isn't able to finish the set. I help nem re-rack the bar. Ne looks like ne could puke, but waves me away.

'I can do this.'

'Nope. You need rest.'

'Make me.'

'If you say so.'

I hook my hands under Gale's armpits and pull nem from the rack with ease. Ne slaps at my sinewy forearms, laughing. Our tomfoolery earns scorn; the powerlifters shoot us dirty looks. For them, the weights room is a place of solemn striving, of force and intensity, proving, *striving*. Someday, over a protein shake, I'll explain that a body is something you're given, not something you're meant to earn.

'What's gotten into you?' I ask Gale, as we prepare my set. Ne loads plates onto the bar, legs still shaky from the squats. Ne starts to say something, thinks better of it, then breathes deep and smiles.

'It's my anniversary!' ne says. 'One year on T, today.'

I shrug—never a meaningless gesture, for me.

'That's it?' Gale slams the last plate onto the bar.

'Half the guys here are on some sort of cocktail, it's not a big deal.'

As I squat, Gale talks, tension untethered, buzzing for an outlet. Ne knows not to talk to me when I'm focused. But ne can't help nemself. Ne lets slip nir gym persona as ne paces, hips rolling, hands gesticulating, the latent theatre kid emerging by way of soliloquy.

'Yes, it's a big deal! I had a speech ready! Who am I kidding, I've hundreds of speeches! All lined up in my head for when I need them. But *this* one was just for you. It was fucking *bespoke*. Just in case I'd read you wrong and you were as bigoted as everyone else. Because who knows? Who ever fucking knows who they're talking to? I don't have a fucking clue why it's so important, you know. What a waste of time. It's a fucking pain that I have to tell everyone fucking else but I thought with you it'd be different, but I didn't know for sure, did I? So I had a fucking speech ready to go and now that you don't care, it's useless.'

I rack the bar with a clang.

'Sounds like a speech to me.'

I show Gale the insides of my elbows, the backs of my knees: track marks galore. It's the same on both my buttcheeks and, if you look close, either side of my scar. I've had more needles in me than I can count.

'You're not the only one with an anniversary, remember.'

Gale checks nemself. 'When's yours?' ne asks.

'Classified.'

'That's not fair.'

'No, it isn't.' I unload weights from the bar for Gale's set and move it down several pegs so that it's at nir height. 'Have you everbbeen to Pink Salt? *Nobody* cares about this sort of stuff.'

Gale folds nir arms. 'I won't come if it's a pity invite.'

'Why would I do that?'

'Because people do. All the time. I don't go out much. Bad experiences. But people tell me I should be putting myself out there. For the *visibility*. Fuck that, I'm no showpony.'

'I didn't say any of that, Gale.'

Ne ignores me.

'Me and the other stagehands have lock-ins. We get drunk, dance. Blues and swing. It's nice. I don't need an audience to have a good time.'

I picture it: a handful of people spinning and sliding across an empty stage, footsteps echoing across rows of empty seats. Whether in spotlit darkness or with the house lights up, to me the image seems lonely, and sad, but I'm not about to yuck nir yum.

Gale tilts nir head, as if testing an idea. 'Ever been in a fight?'

God, I've heard *that* one before. A compliment, a threat, both simultaneously. There's no conceivable use for a body like mine, so impractical and powerful, so demanding. Fit for nothing except to cause damage. People like to test it. To ask only one thing of it.

'No,' I say, and it's the truth.

'Never got into a scrap?'

'Can't put the goods under undue risk. It's in my contract.'

'But you're a bouncer!'

I raise an eyebrow. 'Would you scrap with me?'

Gale laughs. The sound seems to come as a surprise even to nem, and it spins nir tension on its head. Nir posture straightens, nir breathing slows. Ne looks up at the Giantess. The light reflecting off her yellow body gives nir face a sun-lit hue, as if the windowless walls of the weights room have fallen away to reveal blue skies all around.

'Maybe I would, Bruce.' We swap positions in the rack and ne touches a hand to the small of my back. 'Maybe I would.'

'Know what kind of night this is?'

'I think I do, Sally.'

She forces a double take, eyes bulging for effect.

'Sorry, Bruce! Didn't recognise you out of uniform.'

Hard to believe. We're trained to notice difference. Never mind the fact we've stood here together, week-in, week-out, for longer than I'd care to admit; on a basic level of aesthetics, I don't look like anyone else in the queue. My flannel shirt and blue jeans are basic and boring, so committed to their one function, to cover unlikely quantities of skin. Not quite Pink Salt's high-fashion, low-grunge vibe. Maybe Sally thought I'd come to the wrong club; more likely she doesn't like the idea of me being at this particular club for reasons of leisure instead of business.

'Who're you on with?' I ask, wondering who to report for leaving Sally on her own at the door, on this night of all nights.

'Jesus, Bruce, leave the uniform at home for once, will you?'

'What does that mean?'

'It means, take the night off, stop bouncing. Why're you here, anyway?'

'I'm meeting a friend.'

She looks me up and down, then back along the queue of queers.

'What a waste. Go on then.'

Acting as Pink Salt's gatekeeper is one thing, attending is another. As the dance floor fills, I stand by the bar and find myself thinking useless thoughts. This person is femme; that person passes; another, neither. I beat the dull thoughts back, refuse to let them in. Sally's right: I'm off duty, but forever running security. Hunched shoulders relax, stiff hips loosen, white smiles appear in the darkness like rabbits out of hats. Yet even here, people stare. The sheer scale of me, a conversation already closed. In environments like this, bodies like mine are trouble.

'Can I work in?'

Gale appears at my side, bright and nervous. We fumble through a greeting that's one part hug, one part macho shoulder-slap.

'Am I overdressed?' ne asks. Sharp trousers, tap shoes, a shiny shirt held in place under a fidgety bow tie and braces. 'Came straight from work and this was the only thing in the dressing room I didn't hate.'

'I like it. Very Greta Garbo.'

'Shit, too costume-y?'

Three women push past us to the bar, decorative chain-mail breastplates worn over leopard print bodysuits.

'No such thing,' I say.

I get in the first round of drinks. Given the stacks of supplements we're on, neither of us should be boozing, but both of us need to unwind. Pink Salt has other ideas. A man swings towards us on crutches spray-painted gold, glow-sticks woven through the elastic straps of his back brace, his orthopedic shoes doused in glitter. I catch my breath. Without the make-up, wig and cocaine, Glenda looks beyond ill. Gale smiles at him but Glenda doesn't notice.

'Bruce, I want to apologise.' His tone implies I don't have a say in the matter. 'You know what I'm like when I'm in character.' He pauses, expecting me to complete his apology for him. I don't. Gale's smile slips; ne knows something is wrong. 'It's not your fault the institute picked you. Or that I'm too... whatever the fuck I am. I was never going to qualify for treatment. I shouldn't hold that against you.'

He wants forgiveness, but I bite my tongue. After our last encounter, it took me days to feel anything but fake.

Glenda sags on his crutches. 'Please, Bruce, I'm trying to keep the slate clean, I don't want this hanging over me.'

I refuse to give in. I won't do Glenda's heavy lifting for him.

'Fine!' he huffs. 'I had no right. I'm sorry. Okay? I'm sorry.'

Gale looks up at me, an eyebrow raised. I nod. Glenda swings back into the crowd, where friends close ranks around him.

Gale sips nir drink. 'Would you have forgiven them, if I wasn't here?'

'Can we not talk about it?' I say, hoping to halt the interrogation before it begins.

'I don't even know what there is to not talk about.'

'I'd like to keep it that way, too.'

Gale observes me. That's what it feels like. Observation. Like I'm a specimen demonstrating unexpected patterns of behaviour.

'One question,' ne says.

'No.'

I can't bear more questions, can't bear to think of the others who were part of the experiment, those who paved the way, those who I deprived of a second chance. Not tonight. I'm meant to be having a nice time. Tonight, I'm meant to feel normal.

'You don't even know what I want to ask,' says Gale.

But I do know.

It's all anyone ever asks.

Whose body was this?

Against my therapist's advice, I watched the surgery footage. Recorded for posterity, of course. For seven hours and twenty-three minutes, I was nothing more than a severed head up on a surgeon's table, eyes open but unseeing, stump turned to the ceiling, stuck with plastic tubes pumping me full of someone else's blood. I watched the footage over and over, rewinding and pausing, rewinding and pausing, trying to spy the moment I took over someone else's life. Was it the final stitch around my throat? Before that, when their body was wheeled in? When I signed the consent forms? My first heart is dust, my new heart keeps another's beat. Impossible to choose either truth, a lie to believe both.

'Do you dance?'

I blink. The memory of a bright operating theatre dissolves into the dark of a nightclub.

'Hello? Ground control to Bruce? Do you want to dance?'

I'm back in Pink Salt. I'm still here. I never left.

I clear my throat. 'What sort of question is that?'

Gale sets our drinks on the bar and steps one foot between both of mine. 'Widen your stance. Put your weight in your butt with a little tension in your thighs. I feel it in my hips and belly, but I'm guessing you're more chest. Move from there, let everything else follow.'

Before I can protest, Gale dips into the beat. Pressure from nir hand on the back of my hip pulls me close. I try to step away but Gale slides around me, nimble as a spotlight, until we're face to face again. Ne tries to spin me but my body refuses. Another malfunction. Another lifetime ago, another body ago, I'd known how to let this happen, how to move what hurt out of reach, so the beauty of a body could sing. Over nir head I watch other bodies moving in the dark. I envy them, so steady and sure. It can take a whole lifetime for anyone to find their balance.

'I'm not made for dancing.'

Gale laughs. 'Nobody's *made* for anything.'

'You don't understand.' I harden my stance and stop our movements. 'I am. I'm made.'

Ne reaches up to peel back the collar of my shirt. Nir fingers find my scar in the dark. Nir takes my hand and slides it between the buttons on nir shirt. Nir heart beats under nir skin. There's a scar there, too.

I am so tired of tearing myself apart, so that I might repair stronger. The ghost of my old pulse haunts my head. Every fibre, every tendon, every unbreakable bone, so outsized, so useless, so unnatural, all of me floods with calm.

A realisation blooms in my chest, it fills me up like dry ice.

Neither of us know what the other is capable of.

Gale goes on tip-toe, to kiss my scar, to whisper in my ear.

'You're blushing.'

*

When our gym at last evicts The Giantess, it takes half a dozen men to carry her body through the fire exit. They ask me to help, but I refuse. Some days she's the only woman here, and I will not be a part of her disappearance. The men leave her bathing in a skip out back, rainwater collecting in her bolt-holes. The weights room is darker for her loss, and her absent body leaves a faded silhouette, a faint reminder of she who once looked over us.

On the third day, Gale and I reclaim her, and mount her on the wall above our bed.

THE BALLYGILBERT GASSER

deet deet deet

Either Charley or Matty texting him. Nobody else ever did. Graham quit fidgeting with the screws his father had twisted into his bedroom window frame to read the message:

Oh crap, E's mum found out about our tattoos! She's telling your folks at church tomorrow. If there was ever a good time to make good on [1/2]

Charley. Barely anyone they knew had mobiles advanced enough to handle long texts, so Charley's new Samsung S-500, which flipped open on a hinge, snapped all her messages in two and sent them separately, because her texts never came in under 140 characters. Graham would have to wait for the second half to arrive, and sometimes the first half of her texts arrived after the second, and sometimes the second half didn't arrive at all, but still she persisted in using big words, as if it meant something that she refused to talk in shorthand like everyone else in school. He liked this about her, an old-fashioned stubbornness. If he ever did come out to his parents, or decide to run away, Charley could be stubborn for him when he couldn't be stubborn for himself.

A flash of light. Something bright in the middle of the street outside. The beam swept across the contents of his bedroom, as if examining his post-rock posters on the walls, his wardrobe full of ripped denim, the new issue of *Kerrang!* lying open on his bed.

Graham froze, his breath misting on the window. He didn't dare look outside to find the light's source, afraid he might see the illuminated face of the Gilbert Gasser staring back at him.

deet deet deet

[2/2] your getaway plans…

The light moved on. Graham let himself breathe again. Just a passing police car. *You'd think the PSNI would have better things to do,* Graham thought, *than go chasing some urban legend.* The Twelfth was just around the corner. Never mind an invasion of little green men, they'd have their hands full with the Orange sort, the bonfires, the inevitable riots. The Troubles. The never-ending Troubles. Sure the bombs and riots had died down, it was nothing like what his parents lived through, but the threat of regression still hung over Norn Iron like a miasma, a sickening fog. If anyone wanted the violence to stop, Graham's dad always said, they should've named the conflict something simpler, and singular, with a fixed beginning and end. Just call it a civil war. Call it over, it didn't matter who won really, just let it end. But The Troubles, being plural, and present tense, could go on and on for as long as it liked.

He tapped out a reply to Charley.

Wouldn't chuck me out 4 a tattoo. I hope. Not telling them anything til I'm out of this stupid superstitious dump, tho. Where would I go?

He'd room for two more characters.

:)

His nail polish was chipped, probably from pulling at the window screws. He removed a small black bottle from his bedside drawer and, upon opening it, breathed in deep. The acetate odour singed the inside of his nose. This was one of his favourite smells: so unlike itself, so chemical and ugly for something so pretty. He found himself wondering what the Gasser's perfume might smell like, should it visit him later.

The brush swept down over his pinkie nail, replacing the shine. He'd felt like a sissy at first; now he felt exposed if he could see the cuticle beneath the black. He got flak for it at school, but one more year and he could do as he pleased. As the polish dried, Graham looked around his room. It seemed so cramped, so full of *stuff.* Fairy lights above his desk. Incense burning in its paisley-patterned holder by the windowsill. Mogwai on the CD player. This would have been the perfect Saturday night in, if he'd chosen it for himself.

Where else could he go, if he could choose? Anywhere at all—London, New York, Brisbane—as long as his grades were good enough, he could apply for college in Timbuktu if he wanted. Somewhere with just the one flag, that'd be a nice change. Anywhere that wasn't Ballygilbert, Antrim, population a measly 2,000. There'd be more people like him, then.

deet deet deet

hey everyone new number new phone straight from land of rising sun wait til u c it yeer 2000 like nothing uve ever seen luv matty lol

Matty MacReedy. Total legend. Theoretically Matty's phone, a sleek new Japanese model, could read Charley's mammoth texts all in one go, but Matty hadn't been able to make it work now he'd been found and brought back to the UK, and anyway, if there was anything Charley hated more than text-speak, it was talking to Matty. He'd run away at 16, all the way to Tokyo. Nobody heard from him for a year, until his parents paid for a flight home. His adventures made Japan sound more alien than foreign. All the crappy jobs he'd worked with people he couldn't talk to, all the nights he'd slept rough. From a vending machine he'd bought a pair of girly pants, a shiny studded beetle big as his fist, a camera that could change the picture so it looked like a cartoon, or an old-timey photo, anything you wanted. Sounded like bullshit to Graham, but he couldn't prove it. Matty had traded the camera to a stranger in exchange for somewhere to crash, but had to split after the guy started making moves on him. The whole trip, despite the uncertainty and danger, shimmered with the glamour of a life untethered. At least, that's how Matty told it. Graham thought he wanted that.

Then the Gasser came to town. Four foot tall. A squared-off head that glowed like a television set to static. From another planet.

This is how it started. Mrs Dilver, the town librarian, woke one night to find the thing looking in her window. Her bedroom, like Graham's, was on the ground floor, because she could no longer climb the stairs. Through her window, left ajar to circulate the muggy June air, the Gasser had pushed something like a perfume pump to fill her bedroom with white smoke. She'd tried to scream but the smoke had paralysed her. Couldn't squeeze out even a whimper. All the while, the thing's glowing face had shone into the room, casting dead light over her belongings and bedsheets. It pushed the window wide open with its skinny arms, was halfway into the house when her little yapper dog barged into the room and scared it off. She'd lain there for another four hours, unable to move, terrified the thing might come back, the effects of the smoke lifting only when the sun rose.

She told the police first, then the geeks who hung out in the science fiction section of her library, who she'd always doted on, and then *they* told their friends, and then they old their *parents*, and...

Well. Sightings jumped tenfold, identical in detail and execution. Typical Ballygilbert group-think. Nobody around here could think outside themselves to save their lives. It should have ended there, but it didn't. The way the town reacted to the so-called menace, you'd think everyone *wanted* the town plunged into permanent stasis. The police promised to arrest anyone they found skulking around after dusk. Graham's dad went overboard: locks on everything, and the ground floor windows screwed shut. So much for everyone's last summer of being kids. Not that anyone called it that out loud, when adults where nearby. There was an unspoken fear that if their parents overheard, they might decide en-mass that no-one was allowed to grow up after all.

If Graham was an alien looking to abduct folk, he'd start with Belfast or Derry or, heck, even Carrickfergus. He'd touch down on Stormont's newly-minted parliamentary gardens, say 'Take me to your leader,' and laugh as Sinn Fein and the DUP tore chunks out of each other to be first in line for some extra-terrestrial probing. But Ballygilbert? The Gasser was hardly picking the cream of the crop circle here, was he?

deet deet deet

back door left unlocked lol boys n girls cum oot 2 play hunt the gasser matty

Matty, of course, had been questioned by police at the very beginning of the hysteria. He'd been stuck overnight in Belfast, after blagging his way into—and getting kicked out of—a Stiff Little Fingers gig near Queens. What an alibi! Lucky git, always escaping, one way or another.

One afternoon back in second year his biology teacher, Ms Pleath, in very non-committal terms, explained the law, or not quite the law but the threat, of Section 28, how it applied to the relationship between state and school, teacher and pupil. How it limited how much she could tell them about—and here she made eye contact with Graham, held it just a little too long—alternative lifestyles. If Ms Pleath could single him out like that, he wasn't as subtle as he liked to believe.

It had been four years since he'd admitted it to himself. Four years since he'd stood in front of the mirror in the bathroom and whispered words at his reflection. *Woofter. Sissy. Fag.* Four years he'd waited to get out of Ballygilbert and find out for himself if another future could exist. Matty and Charley and everyone else could leave home with a guarantee they could remain who they already were, that who they already were could be who they wanted to be, that who they wanted to be needed no tweaking.

Not him. He would change, for sure.

The night stretched out like old chewing gum. The smell of polish faded. The Mogwai CD spun into silence. Graham got up and stood at his bedroom door, under the Godspeed poster. He'd take take it with him when he left for college, or an apprenticeship, along with the others: Low, Explosions in the Sky, Trail of Dead. The only parts of himself he'd be content continuing beyond Ballygilbert came with ready-made fanbases and online forums, spaces he could occupy without first having to explain himself, or so he hoped.

He listened at the door, then peeked out into the downstairs hallway. Empty. He went to the wobbly computer table by the front door, the one spot in the house with a phone line connected to The Internet. Maybe he could catch someone from school moan about being under house arrest, using the private chatroom they set up in I.T. that day they had a substitute teacher who wasn't paying attention.

bddbddbddbddbddbdd, gargled the dial-up. *Glaaaaa—chkchk—pdapdapdapda—aiiieewwhoooooo—dip dip dip.*

'Graham, honey!' From upstairs, his mum shouted down at him. 'I'm on the line to Tina, can you wait a moment? Sorry, Tina, Graham's trying to get on The Internet. Hello? Graham, shut it off!'

He tried not to slam his bedroom door. He really did.

deet deet deet

Oh my god, did u get Matty's text? Gonna be so much trouble. What if police find him? He's so dense. You can have him. Seriously. Such a li [1/2]

Everyone fancied Matty. Even Charley. Maybe especially Charley.

Matty might not use big words, but he knew big places. He'd seen a world outside of Ballygilbert that Charley could only read about. Beyond Belfast, where on weekends they'd all loiter outside City Hall with the goths, and shout, and smoke. Charley had sewn a secret fag pouch into Graham's backpack, and if this was any other Saturday night he would be sneaking a ciggie out the open window. If only he could get the screws out from the window frame. But they stood slightly raised and motionless under his painted fingers.

He would try again come morning, pry them out with the aid of a hammer. With his parents at church, he could make as much noise as he wanted.

Some of his classmates suspected the Gasser was some dipshit first year, but that didn't make sense. They'd have to know the school's chemistry lab inside-out to make their paralysis fog. They'd need skills in woodworking and electronics, to make the glowing headpiece. And they'd have to be psychotic to try something this audacious in such a small town. No kid he knew was that diligent, that unbalanced.

deet deet deet

[2/2] *ability.*

Maybe—and this was the scary part, to Graham—the Gasser wasn't a kid messing about with school supplies. The Gasser might be an adult. A grown-up, running around town trying to break into people's houses and… what? What then? Some people, when their parents stopped holding them close, just fell apart. As if they'd not had enough time or love or hope to solidify into a proper human being. What would someone like that be able to do?

Graham wondered if that might someday happen to him.

If it hadn't happened already.

Outside, the cruising police car made another round, pulsing through the dark in silence. Graham dropped down onto his bed to flip through his music mag some more. By midnight he'd read every word twice, no closer to feeling tired. On tiptoe he stepped into the hallway, sat down at the computer with a concentrated grace. Puberty made being quiet so difficult. It seemed every day he'd earned new bruises from bumping into things, his stretched and lanky frame taking different shapes from week to week. He took off his t-shirt and wrapped it around the bulky black box of the modem. Perhaps the padding would—

ddbddbddbddbddbddbdddglaaaachkchkchkipdipdip

'Graham! Go to bed! It's late!'

This time he slammed his bedroom door as hard as he could. After a few minutes he heard his dad come downstairs to double-check the locks on the front door, then the back. They didn't trust him. That was the real reason why the computer was in the corridor—a land line could be installed *anywhere* in the house, even his bedroom, but then how would they check on him? They were so scared of The Internet, but it wasn't a classroom they could shush, or a postal service they could monitor. It was a giant playground filled with countless cliques and weird kids and proof of weirder, scarier things than anyone could imagine.

deet deet deet

O M G guys i saw it

Graham rolled his eyes. Perhaps across town Charley was rolling hers as well. He tapped out a reply:

Yeah right, Matty. And you ate live squid and shagged a geisha in a karaoke booth. You're so full of CRAP.

deet deet deet

no look i got a pic

error: unable to open file

That was new. Graham exited his phone's inbox folder then tried to re-open Matty's message, but got the error message again.

Whatever you're sending me it's not showing up.

deet deet deet

not lying! OMG man it glows in the head

error: unable to open file

MATTY. What are you trying to send me. It won't work.

deet deet deet

sending pics phones got a camera told u yeer 2000

deet deet deet

Why do we let him get away with this, G? I bet you any money he's still in the house watching Blind Date with his dad. He's boring & bluffing [1/2]

Charley and her big words.

Graham rubbed the phone's buttons as if trying to convince it to show him the text's second half. God help her if she was ever in serious danger. Three minutes passed, and still no completion. In a fit of impatience Graham threw the issue of *Kerrang!* across his room. It slapped against the wardrobe. The impact dislodged a piece of clothing inside. In a few months he'd have to trade all his band t-shirts and torn jeans for white shirts and neat suits, he'd have to go to *job interviews.*

deet deet deet

[2/2] just like the rest of us.

deet deet deet

its moving towards charleys street
Why tell me? Tell her! Call the police!

deet deet deet

so u believe me
I will if you call the police. They can catch him.

deet deet deet

g man it's not a him i dont know what it is
Come off it, Matty. You're a lying douchebag and it's not funny. Not everyone gets to have the life you do and you're rubbing it in our faces so if you are out there with the Gasser call the police because this is my last summer of being young, OK?

Couldn't send, too long. Graham tried to edit it down.

Come off it Matty, you're lying, you're not funny. Not everyone has your life and you're rubbing it in our faces so if you're out there with the Gasser call the police and let us enjoy our last summer.

Still too much. Cut it back, cut it back.

Matty not funny not every1 has ur life ur rubbin our faces in it if ur out there n it is call polis save our summer

Gibberish. That's how Ballygilbert worked, chopping bits off, until you stopped making sense even to yourself. Graham decided not to send the text, but saved it to his drafts folder it to show Charley on Monday in class. They'd laugh about it, and things would feel normal for a bit.

deet deet deet

its at charleys house
error: unable to open file

```
deet deet deet
```
Matty's a pain in the ass.
```
deet deet deet
```
see its head glowing

error: unable to open file
```
deet deet deet
```
He's scaring the shit out of me, Graham.
```
deet deet deet
```
error: unable to open file

OLLY I CAN'T DO ANYTHING
```
Deet deet deet
```
[2/2] help!

And sometimes—*sometimes*—Charley's phone sent the second half of her texts without sending the first.

Graham lifted his *Kerrang!* from the floor. He looked at it without seeing the pictures or reading the words. He checked his phone once, twice, five times. No new messages. Matty was only fooling around. Wasn't he? Matty's attachment still wouldn't open. Cameras inside phones—what would that even look like? How did they find the space for the lens, the shutter, the other parts of a camera Graham couldn't name even if he tried? Matty was ahead of everyone, always. That's why Graham and Charley never told Matty where to go. He was probably already there.

Graham sent Charley a text:

So what happened?

Without waiting for an answer, he tried again:

What's going on?

Nothing.

Matty's lying, he told himself. There's no alien with a glowing head breaking into people's homes, paralysing them with smoke.

But if—

The forensic flash of a police car swept his room once more, this time calling Graham to the window. He studied the quiet, curfewed street.

—if there was—

He looked at his phone, silent. He looked at the screws in the window frame. He prodded the splinters squeezed out of the wood with his thumb and gasped when one pricked him.

—if something was out there—

He tried calling Charley, even though he couldn't spare the minutes. No answer. He had to get to Charley, and Matty. Even if everything was normal, he had to get out, or everything wouldn't actually be okay.

—snatching people away—

He pulled the Godspeed poster off his bedroom door and plucked the blu-tack from its corners. Rolling the sticky stuff into a ball, he moulded it over one of the screws in the window, pressing it into the head's groove.

—he'd say—

Then he tore strips of stiff, glossy paper from *Kerrang!* and scrunched them around the blu-tac, for better grip. He pressed. He pinched. He twisted. A minute felt like light-years, but slow, and slight, the screw turned in the wood. His hands shook.

—he'd say—

He chipped a nail, pulling out the last screw.

—Take me first.

The window popped open. A gust of wind toppled his incense stick to the floor. Graham swore under his breath as he stamped the ash into the carpet to stop it burning. Night air moved around him, sucked the sweet smoke into the darkness. He could climb out onto his front lawn, simple as that. He could intercept the Gasser, stand in its cool light, huff whatever paralysing vapours it offered, and say, *take me.*

Or he could hitch-hike to the airport, catch a flight to Tokyo, forbidden pleasures, impossible technology.

Or he could walk to Belfast, reach City Hall by dawn and wait for the skaters and rockers to congregate, like they did every weekend.

Or he could stay here, wait for the police to sweep by again.

Or he could do nothing. And that would be okay, too.

deet deet deet

OMG. Dad just caught Matty running around outside with a flashlight. Police are on their way. I'm not joking, that boy needs some psychiatric [1/2]

Graham stood there until his skin broke out in goosebumps. He looked around his bedroom, examining its contents. What a mess. The Mogwai poster lay face down on the floor. His copy of Kerrang was shredded. His incense stained the carpet grey. The window frame was splintered and cracked and the screws wouldn't go back in tight. Maybe his dad wouldn't notice, and his mum wouldn't ask what he was doing, going on The Internet in the middle of the night. Maybe in a few years he'd tell them about that time he almost ran away, and they'd laugh, or shrug, or they wouldn't even be on speaking terms and it would be exactly as if he'd not chosen to stay and they'd never know.

Whatever happened next, there was no stopping it. He just had to wait to meet it, and stay sane.

OTHER LANDSCAPES ARE POSSIBLE

1.

Hot napalm drips in patient rivers from palms and fronds, jungle vegetation curling green and blue to ash. Slow birds erupt from foliage, wings evaporating as they scream into the smoke to thud against the low ceiling of the shrinking sky. A panther, or soot-slicked leopard, some big cat with ears laid flat, lopes across the blackening scrub. Destruction, indiscriminate.

Judith adjusts the stolen flame-thrower's shoulder straps and squeezes off another jet of terrible light, a hot whip laid upon the night. She feels no remorse.

It is not a real night. Not even a real jungle. This environment is a patchwork of lies. It's the accumulation of what a jungle should be.

By her side, The First Man cowers.

He crouches and pulls his matted hair and slaps his shimmering chest. Judith wants to calm him, wants to hold his head and see him bare his teeth in pleasure one last time, but his face is no longer his own. His features writhe and change, like blue smoke across a full, fake moon. This was their spot. Where they'd first met. Judith wants it to be the first to burn.

It's strange, how the genuine flame intersects with the edges of this made-up universe: coated in burning truth, the fake microcosm melts like a communion wafer. Not even the ash remains.

She hopes the other woman escapes before everything disappears; she deserves more than this perfect broken world.

2.

'Well? Where is it?' General MacInnes sat opposite her in the long cargo hold of the Chinook, his impatience counting down like a grenade with the pin pulled out. 'Show us this *Eden* of yours.'

Said with spite, as if she'd come up with the name, but that's what the military chose to call her impossible paradise. No surprise there. Men point at things and name them without first asking what they might be, and lose their temper when you tell them they're wrong.

'I did say, a ground approach would be easier.' She kept her tone even and reasonable. Either nobody in the corridors of power had believed her report, or they'd not bothered to read it. A lot of work had gone into that report. 'The land looks different from up here.'

The Cairngorms appeared strange when seen from the air, for sure, but for Judith they held a new richness that turned her stomach. Since returning from Eden, everything real was abrasive, too full of information. Something so simple as a glass of water had become complex, each sip like sandpaper on her tongue, flavoured with a history of permafrost, wild heather and reindeer shite. The Chinook tilted in the cloudless summer sky. Alongside them, smaller helicopters flew in formation. Below, Ben Macdui rearranged itself.

'There.' Judith pointed at a grassy clearing in the scrub next to a body of water.

'This better be our last stop,' said MacInnes. 'This isn't *Snow White.*'

'Excuse me?'

'We can't keep checking all your hunches until we find the right spot, can we?'

Did he mean *Goldilocks*, Judith wondered? 'That isn't...'

'Isn't what?' growled MacInnes. 'Go on, tell me what it isn't.'

'Nothing. It's nothing.' How could he be so unfamiliar with *Snow White?* The fairy tale was nearly as universal as Eden. It didn't matter, though, they'd found the right spot, she was sure this time. On a solo trek the year before, she'd pitched her tent in that exact clearing and dallied for a few days in solitude until two men came along. They nodded hello and set up camp. She packed up and set off. It was safer to keep moving.

She sighed. Did that have to be the reason why she remembered the anomaly's location so clearly? Not the mind-bending discovery, not the serene calm of a tarn in May, but... a fear of men?

MacInnes' anger was a live grenade. Judith's was a fully-stocked silo.

They touched down. The soldiers unloaded their scuba gear and guns, their inflatable tents. She'd given them no guarantee their equipment would survive the journey from reality to Eden, but the Ministry of Defence considered the existence of a pocket dimension an issue of border control, and required forces secure the region.

An hour's uphill climb felt much longer with rifles pointed at her back. She distracted herself with memories of the first time she took this trek. The first time she found the caves with icy ceilings, and the cool standing water inside. Its surface had curdled at her outstretched fingertips. A restless shimmer, like the northern lights when they came this far south, had beckoned her into the pool, pulled her deeper and deeper until gravity flipped her around and she rose again, the water now sun-warm, her heart fit to burst.

Perhaps Eden was as good a name as any.

Perhaps *Snow White* and *Goldilocks* were the same story.

Anything for an easy life.

3.

It felt like love. No, it felt love-adjacent: *adoration*. A feeling too vast to define, it filled her up and flooded the empty spaces between atoms in her body. It felt like coming home, prodigal and safe. Every inch of Eden was a new discovery that somehow felt familiar. Each species of fern or lily or sprouting bean was brand new. Fat ladybirds adorned impeccable leaves. Birdsong sounded almost intelligible. It was exactly as one might expect a primordial green to look and smell and feel, if you weren't familiar with the chaos of nature. The air was thick with the joy of everything being as it should, always was, ever would be.

Everything but for The First Man.

He simply couldn't be real. He was an absurd Tarzan. Uncorrupted. Gym-fit. Salon-smooth. Not a single pimple on His angled hairless jaw.

Articulate in His movement. His odour awakened in Judith an ache to sprint to the horizon in the hope the world was flat, and they were alone to start anew.

And He was very white. That was the strangest thing. She was reluctant to define Him as Caucasian, not least because she knew from her studies the Caucasus mountains were in the Middle East. Not albino, either, more an elfish, unearthly pale. At any rate, the jungle treated Him like a White Man. Swarms of biting flies moved out of his way. Palm trees shook coconuts into His outstretched palms. Whatever He needed, the jungle provided, no questions asked.

After their first tryst, Judith and The First Man lay on their backs in the grass and stared up at the black sky. No stars, no Mars, no Jupiter. Of course not. There'd never been a big bang here. The solar system as she knew it, was nothing more than detritus from a different beginning, one that had no bearing on paradise.

Still, she told Him where the constellations would have been, if they'd been camping in the Cairngorms. He understood everything she said, and didn't talk back. That was Judith's first big clue that this world was unreal. The First Man never tried to tell her anything she already knew.

Well, that, and he didn't ever seem to need to shit.

It was all too perfect, a faultless simulacrum of one perfect beginning in a pantheon of thousands. There were no sphinxes or gorgons in this jungle, no elemental yin and yang. Things just were, and were right, except for Judith, who made for a lacklustre Eve. The scholar in her knew, she should examine every inch of this impossible place with utmost scepticism, but that felt like touching an ancient fresco that had somehow not yet dried, impossible but untouchable.

This studied ignorance excused her from examining the Other Thing that called this paradise home, which Judith refused to look at, and refused to recognise.

4.

Judith's second dive, chaperoned by Her Majesty's Finest, felt sacrilegious. Well, as much as you could betray something you didn't believe in. There was no way she could have known what she was doing, the scale of the threat she was guiding to Eden, or what they'd do to The First Man when the military found him. And they would find him. Eden wasn't that big.

Please, she'd thought as she kicked towards the portal, *don't be so basic as to wait for me.*

But there he was on the other shore, naked and flawless and waiting for her. Pitched against the most recent version of Man, The First didn't stand a chance. MacInnes and his soldiers took the beach in formation, thrust the business ends of their guns in the innocent idiot's face, shouted orders. He understood them, and didn't talk back.

General MacInnes hauled her on-shore with a hand around her throat. 'You didn't tell us there were natives!' he shouted. He directed his forces into the jungle in groups of three and four with orders to hunt down hostiles. 'What else haven't you told us?'

Judith looked at the grains of sand stuck to her bare feet, then up at MacInnes' blotchy face. She said nothing. The back of his hand connected with her cheek. She sucked fresh blood off her gums. The First Man struggled against his inferiors and made a sharp keening noise, like an otter in distress. MacInnes looked between The First Man and Judith, and began to laugh. 'Fucking typical,' he said. 'Think you're clever? Let me show you what happens to clever girls and the goody-two-shoes who fuck them.'

He ordered men to pitch a gigantic hunk of driftwood in the sand like a post, and bound her to it, arms pinned behind her back with cable ties at the wrist. He made her watch as the inflatable tents *fwoomped* into shape on the golden shore. Within an hour (and was that not sacrilegious in itself, bringing the concept of time to this neverland?) the military had re-purposed their medical centre as an interrogation cell. Sharp instruments glinted in the sourceless sun.

They unpacked The First Man infinitely. They were able to turn him this way and that to find new penetralia. He was nothing more to them than a concept.

But how he howled, how he howled, how he howled.

5.

Judith woke to wild electronic birdsong. Gunshots rattled across the beach. A noise like snapped celery. Spotlights at her feet revealed bodies, unmade during the night, and a dance of reptilian footprints leading away into the base. The smell of blood and perfume hung in the air. There, beyond the perimeter: a glint of green scales under floodlights, two slit eyes glowing yellow in the dark. Down on all fours, the shadow skittered towards her.

The Other Woman.

Judith couldn't help herself. She screamed and kicked, called for help. She retched at the other woman's touch. She was ashamed at her own disgust, but the stench was so strong up close, red roses and rotting meat. The other woman's cold, sharp hands clawed at the cable ties around her wrists, but couldn't break through the plastic.

With a grunt, the other woman levered the driftwood out of the sand and dragged it to the water's edge, taking Judith with her. The pool closed around Judith's bound ankles, then her knees. She tilted her head to face the starless sky. Bullets peppered the waves. Her wooden stump rolled. She came up gasping, just the once, before the other woman dove, and pushed down, towards the beckoning light of reality.

6.

Deep inside Ben Macdui, the extraction team watched Judith crawl from the cave's waters, alone. Though she'd spent less than a day in Eden, their military buzzcuts had grown out, wisps of auburn hair curling from under their helmets. Back in the helicopter, Judith observed her pilot as he radioed ahead their arrival. Were his lips more luscious? Five miles outside Edinburgh, her government escort stood taller, if possible, in his plain suits and dark sunglasses. Over the course of a two-day interrogation in a featureless room, her interrogator's skin lightened several shades and showed no sign of stopping.

This time she told all, from start to finish. There was no point holding back, the damage was done. A year ago she'd found an idea in the mountains. She lived in it for a time, and it was perfect, but that's all it was. She came back to reality hungry for imperfection, but found so much of it she thought she was losing her mind. So she asked for help from the wrong people, who saw perfection as a threat, a resource waiting to be plundered. She included The First Man in this new telling, and got a small thrill from detailing how the Other Woman had ripped through the Ministry's forces with nothing but her bare hands.

The men listened to her story. Then they injected her with something that made the world go wobbly and left her on the cobbled streets of Stockbridge, in nothing but her bloodstained expedition gear. She was lucky it was summer. In her druggy stupor, the mild air was kind to her skin the way it used to be, before Eden had spoiled her.

Judith's wits returned, but her old life did not. With flawless white smiles, bank tellers informed her there were no records of an account in her name. Friends pretended not to know her, their identical blue eyes ringed with fear. A strange family now lived in her flat and they all wore their hair long and free.

By the time she found a night shelter, the priests in charge looked like menswear models, dog collars tight around throats newly corded with muscle. After lights out, one stood by her flimsy bed until she invited him under the rough covers. He was generous and attentive and extremely unlikely.

The next morning, she woke alongside a stranger she recognised. He took her to a nearby greasy spoon and over sandpapery tea and toast they watched the news on his phone. The Prime Minister stood outside Downing Street and announced World Peace. She looked like the First Man, and over the course of her ten minute speech she outgrew her ugly blue pant-suit. The newsreader looked like the First Man too, studio make-up clownish on her flawless skin. She joked about having nothing to report before handing over to her correspondent in George Square, Glasgow, where the 29th Glasgow Scout Group sung hymns, their identical dicks showing obscene under their child-sized kilts.

This must be what happens, she supposed, if you dissect an ideal man seeking answers, instead of questions.

Whoever she'd left behind in Eden had learned something useful about being a man, and used it to create a feedback loop of ideology.

Nobody was alarmed by this sweeping regulation of Homo Homogenic. At the greengrocers, the train station, the library and the sushi bar, The First Man listened to her woes and took her home and fucked her like she wanted, and afterwards nothing more was expected of her.

There were worse hells to endure.

7.

Truth is, the First Man had not been Judith's first Edenic encounter. She'd been sat on the sand wringing water from her hair when she felt something watching her with a steady, yellow-eyed gaze. It was not curious, not concerned, not surprised. It wanted to watch. Viewed head-on, it was flat-faced and monstrous, dark scales pushing through the skin to slough off in palm-wide segments.

Yet when Judith looked out across the water, keeping her companion in corner-vision, the creature appeared pretty, in a conventional sort of way. Which was to say, white and skinny and woman and human. Judith couldn't be certain, because whenever she turned to look directly at the other woman, the supermodel effect disappeared, but she was convinced the pretty version wore fig leaves bunched up around its crotch, with nothing to hold them there but the bloody-minded optimism of modesty.

When both women become used to each other's presence, the horrid thing advanced on Judith with a smile made to catch rodents.

Judith ran from her, straight into the open arms of the First Man.

8.

On her third day in hell Judith woke up screaming with a forked tongue from a nightmare she couldn't remember. Later, in a stranger's bathroom, watching her reflection's pupils lengthen to slits, she remembered how the trees shook their bounty into the First Man's outstretched palms, how the jungle gave him everything he wanted without asking anything in return.

It wasn't fair.

9.

Her third dive was easy. The military drove her out to Ben Macdui where the military team, all identikit, carried her to the caves like a queen without argument or conflict. They kitted her out with a wetsuit and oxygen tank and wished her the best, but went no further than the edge of the pool. It seemed The First Man would do anything for her, except go back to where he came from.

On the other side, blood on the shore glued perfect granules of sand into brown-black clods. The camp was ruined. Plastic shreds of inflatable tents flapped in the treetops. One remaining containment unit wheezed with life.

She wasn't ready to see what it held, but she looked anyway.

'Beautiful, isn't it?' said a voice.

A man stepped from the tree line, clothed in muddy military fatigues. She took note of the machete tucked into his belt, and wondered if military-grade wetsuits were knife-proof. He looked like The First Man, but he could've been anybody.

'What did you do to him?' she asked.

'We took him apart,' said the person. He moved to stand near her at a respectful distance. 'Then we put him back together.'

Judith looked again at the thing inside the containment unit. The First Man's body shifted against itself. Interior forces stretched his hips, passed melanin variations across his skin like shadows across a field. Semblances of others rose from beneath to bubble on the surface of his face then sink. His his nose flattened then snubbed, his ears stretched, his eyes flickered blue, green, grey, each colour flooded with confusion. In tearing into him, mankind had left behind something of themselves. Conceptual contamination. Once the idea of a man, now the idea of many, his body couldn't contain multitudes.

Did his mind warp, too? Could he remember her? Their time together? Judith couldn't tell. She placed a hand on the unit's window, in the hope that he might raise his own to mimic her. He looked at the hand as if it had never once stroked his face, or held his wrists to the ground in the night. It was apt for an idea of humanity to flux and flip and not know itself from moment to moment. This was closer to the truth.

Still, he was nothing compared to his companion. They'd pulled her apart, and left her like that. The absolute *bastards*.

'We put ourselves back together,' said the man. He kept his distance. 'Like *Humpty Dumpty*.'

Judith shook to the ground with cold laughter. She knew who he was now, who he really was. 'That's not how that story goes,' she said. 'You should've studied the humanities, MacInnes.'

'Don't call me that.' He moved closer. 'I'm not that person.'

'Fuck off.'

He moved closer still. 'I'm sorry I slapped you. That was unkind.'

'What do you know,' she sneered, 'of kindness?'

He stood over her. He placed his hand on her shoulder, and through the fabric of her wetsuit she felt his grip tighten.

'Let me show you.'

He smelled good. God-dammit, *he smelled good*.

When Judith was finished, she stuck the machete into the sand. She held the General's decapitated head by the hair. He looked like The First Man, but he could have been anybody.

She pressed it against the containment unit's window for the Other Woman to see. She smiled her sharp smile, and Judith smiled back.

10.

The flamethrower chokes out one last fiery tongue before the tank runs dry. Judith shrugs it off and retreats towards the pool, dragging the First Man with her. She goes too far, or not far enough, or the path folds back on itself. Through the smoke she picks out a high point of land, fixates on it as best she can. Grass gives way to rubble, and they begin to climb. Four times they pass the exact same boulder covered in blackened moss, though she has circled the hill once, if that.

At the peak, all becomes clear. This world is an idea of a world, the First Man an idea of a man, and as man's idea of Man collapses into similitude, so too does his Eden. You can see where the seams flip segments of the jungle back in on itself like a kaleidoscope, trees and shrubs slotting together like pieces of a cardboard diorama, or collapsing origami. The smokey air shifts, and buzzes. Swarms of flies rise to crowd the tessellating sky with billions wings and compound eyes.

In the distance, the pool shrinks down to a puddle. Ripples close over two clawed feet kicking their way into reality. Eden folds into itself one last time, its dense perfection crushed into nothing. And good for her, thinks Judith, just before she stops existing.

Good for her.

THE
OFFSET AND THE CALVING

Beyond Iceland's Ring Road border of Alaskan lupins, tall and bulbous purple, a fat plume of steam puffed from distant rocks to blend into the low clouds, and Edith imagined the entire world somewhere between a snow globe and crystal ball. She could shake it, and peer inside, and see herself tossed around, to settle into an unknown future.

'It's so fucking pretty,' she said to June, who was driving them to an ice lagoon. In the steady morning light June's round face looked thinner than the face Edith had fallen for, in another time, in a different country. Edith shifted her seatbelt to a more comfortable position across her stomach and wondered if an Icelandic lifestyle would have a similar effect on her own stubborn body, too fond of bad habits.

'They're invasive,' said June. 'The lupins. Brought here ages ago. They're making it difficult for other plants.'

Edith laughed. 'Can we at least get out of town before we crash into reality, Captain buzzkill?'

'I thought it was interesting!' June kept her eyes on the road. 'The steam over there's a geothermal plant. Or hydroelectric?'

'You've been here how long and you still don't know?' said Edith,

'Oh, come on. Where's your nearest power plant, back home?'

There was something in how June said '*home*' which suggested her definition of the word had, in the last year, cleaved away from Edith's. You could tell just to look at the two of them. Edith wore hiking boots, old jeans and a bright waterproof jacket, as advised by dozens of tourist websites. Meanwhile June looked as normal and at home as everyone else in Reykjavík, wrapped up in simple layers.

'How far away is Juka... Julaca...'

'Jökulsárlón? Three hours, maybe four.'

'Wow, that's longer than it took to fly here.'

'Correct,' said June in a tone that suggested Edith had in fact said something wrong. The roads were long and straight and challenging in their constancy. 'You've got me doing the tourist circuit.'

'Thank you, again.'

'It's okay,' said June. 'Haven't been to the lagoon since I first got here.'

'Yeah, well, thanks.'

'You don't have to keep saying it.'

She'd been unfair on June, showing up unannounced at her work, a store that sourced clothing from artists and crafters all along the Arctic circle and sold it as high fashion. The shop staff ushered her into a basement stuffed with half-finished suits, string, tape and sewing machines. June hadn't been angry to see her. A clipboard of spreadsheets tucked under her arm, she'd scribbled Edith a map to her house. As if she'd forgotten how bad Edith was at spatial things like reading maps. As if she didn't care that Edith had avoided looking at maps since June left. Because now Edith hated maps. The time difference wasn't too difficult to manage between Iceland and Scotland, but the *distance* distance? All that sea, all those underwater ridges and salt-water clefts? Over months the knowledge of them gathered up into its own impasse, rising from the depths.

After so much silence, and such a practical welcome, Edith was thankful June hadn't asked her to sleep on the sofa. Instead, in June's bed of pale wood and light blue sheets, they'd spooned until they fell asleep. Just spooning, June's nose to the nape of Edith's neck, June's warm hands holding Edith's soft belly. Nothing else happened. Neither of them wanted it. Everything between them was fragile, too easily bruised.

But here in the car on the road to Jökulsárlón June seemed to have frosted solid overnight.

'So are you going to tell me?' she asked. 'We can stop avoiding it, right?'

'Avoiding what?'

'Whatever you couldn't put in a short email.'

'You've been busy. Y'know, sorting yourself out here.'

'I've been here eleven months, Edie. I'm pretty well sorted.'

No surprise there. Swapping a career in Scottish arts funding for a sales job in Icelandic fashion had seemed as simple for June as washing off a face mask. Edith knew the truth wasn't that simple—it took a lot of energy to appear so collected—but couldn't shake the feeling that June led a frictionless life. When she accelerated to overtake three other cars, first one pulled over to the side of the road, then another, then the last, each one full of tourists stopping for photos of a collection of stone cairns among the lupins.

'Tell me what's going on,' June said. 'You owe me that.'

So as the geothermal plumes faded in the rear-view mirror, Edith vented. The short version was this: She'd lost her job in the print shop. They'd been kind enough to pay her the full month's salary, so she'd bought a flight to Iceland. Why not? If her whole life could become shifting sand, it made sense to run towards solid ground. June was solid—wasn't she?

'I assume,' said June, 'the long version elaborates on why they fired you?'

The car crested a ridge, bringing into view a complex of ghost-white, low ceilinged buildings, dwarfed but bright against the rolling expanse of dark rock.

'What're those?'

'You're deflecting.'

'Are they greenhouses?'

Could June drive for hours and not once feel the need to comment on such outlandish scenery?

'*Edith*. Answer me. Isn't printing just pressing buttons?'

'Okay, yeah,' Edith huffed. 'I fucked up.'

Printers, creasers, guillotines. Such old inventions, you'd think they were simple. Not so. Centuries of evolution had heaped complexity upon complexity, transforming basic processes into magic tricks. Calibrations of half a millimetre, applied to one teeny tiny toty sensor hidden deep in the clunking, whirring innards of a machine could pull everything back into alignment, make everything right. When the heartless things broke down, men in grease-spattered overalls would hold striped sheets up to the light, pointing out errors so inconsequential Edith often had to lie and say she could see what the problem was even when she couldn't. Worst of all had been clearing paper jams, when for no good reason the greedy things would gobble several sheets in one go, clogging their gears and rollers, as if self-sabotaging. The solution was to pinch and tease with tweezers, delicate and patient, until the obstruction cleared. Edith's preferred method was to stick her big hands in among the small things, grab and yank and hope for the best. Sometimes things ripped and snapped. Expensive things.

She looked over at June, who was smiling to herself, eyes still focused on the long road ahead.

'Let's take a detour,' said June. 'It'll set us back an hour but you'll get a kick out of it. There should be a map in the glove compartment. Get it out.'

Edith did as directed, too surprised by the change of plan to resent how easy it was to obey June, and be reshaped.

On either side of the rift, the red-brown walls of the North Atlantic Ridge stood thirty feet tall. June walked ahead on the boardwalk laid down between the cliffs, eager to complete the detour as soon as possible, but Edith dallied. She felt like a marble lost between old, warped floorboards.

'I can't believe they just let people walk down here,' she said. 'Isn't it still moving?'

'Seven millimetres every year.'

'Fuck! That's an entire bleed area!'

June looked back at the car park, then at her watch. 'A what?'

Edith had hoped the jargon she'd learnt could be spat out of her head like an ash cloud, but no such luck. Somewhere inside, it had fused to her, and she was now forever going to be surprised at the scale of things. A stack of posters trimmed a whole seven millimetres short were destined for the recycle bin. But here, where America and Eurasia rubbed rocky shoulders, two giants sliding against each other hot and sharp? Inconsequential.

'Space between artworks on a sheet, for when we're trimming off...'

June's face was a bluff, she didn't care.

'Sweetie?' she said, foot tapping.

'This was your idea.'

'It's just rocks. I'd like to be home by midnight.'

Strapped back into the passenger seat, Edith found herself envying the tectonic plates' lack of concern for the delicacy of people. After an hour of driving, invasive wildflowers gave way to acres of old lava, folded in on itself in solid black bubbles, all coated with light-green moss.

'This is amazing,' said Edith. It made her feel a little ill. 'It's like curdled milk on burnt toast.'

'I go this route once a month, we've a buyer in Fjarðabyggð.'

The road was narrow and rubbled at the edges. The speedometer read in kilometres rather than miles, so Edith had no idea how fast they were going, but what baffled her was when the road would bend and change direction. What was the reason? Why not fly straight ahead, what impossible terrain had decided they should turn left, or right, or rise above it all on buzzing cage-metal bridges?

'I don't think I could ever be bored here.'

'You only got in yesterday,' said June. 'You've barely started your holiday.'

'I'm not on holiday.'

The car's tyres scrabbled in the black dirt at the side of the road, and June pulled it back towards the centre line.

'You're not?'

'No.'

June turned on the radio. After they passed through the lava fields the signal became patchy, the presenter's voice fragmented into shards of language Edith didn't understand enough to piece together. June turned the radio off, which was worse. It took effort to break the stillness, but there was still wonder in the journey and Edith would not let it go unremarked upon. 'I mean, those mountains! They're shaped like... a sleeping dragon! Can you see it? A head, down to a neck, then back up into a chest and wings. The snout's pointing towards the road.'

'There's a nice waterfall on the other side. Skógafoss.'

'Jeez, spoilers much?'

The bouldered beast filled their view from their little tin can of a car. No need to breathe flame if ever it took flight: hot air rushing from under its mile-wide shadow would cloak it in lightning, storms and fury. They rounded the snout. The crashing waters of Skógafoss shone in the afternoon glare, a shimmering tinfoil panel set into earth.

'Nice?' said Edith. 'Nice is nothing! That's magnificent! There's a road! Can we? Can we please?'

'Maybe on the way back.'

'We'll be too tired.'

'I'm not your tour guide.'

'What?'

'I said,' said June, 'I'm not your fucking tour guide.'

'Pull over.'

'I'm *not* stopping.'

Edith's fists clenched of their own accord. The rushing sound she heard could have been Skogafóss or the blood in her ears.

'I don't mean for the waterfall, June.'

June sighed. 'Hold on. There's a lay-by just ahead.'

By 'just ahead', she meant another twenty minute drive. The lush mountains crumbled into miles of black sand and grey rubble, aeons old ash. Edith's fury cooled from white hot to a liquid red, crusted over with dark resignation. She was just one angry person, buzzing away in the middle of nowhere. She thought about what it must be like to drive this road twice a month.

Had something similar had happened to June, with what had once been between them? Wonderment burnout: Feelings fizzling to nothing when presented with so much time and space and indescribable beauty. Petty love held out to the stars, unimpressed.

June turned off-road into a gravelled lay-by and parked next to a picnic bench. There was no other evidence of humanity in sight. Everything felt so futile. They sat inside the car in silence until Edith couldn't take it anymore. She got out of the car and screamed. It was windier out here than she had expected, and more full of flies. She waved the bugs away from her mouth and felt silly. June shut the engine off and stepped out of the car.

'Feel better?'

'No.'

'Sort of stops right in front of your face, doesn't it? Nothing for the sound to bounce off.'

'It's scary.'

They sat down at the table, facing each other, June's expression unreadable.

'What were you expecting?'

'Not an echo. But not that either.'

'No. From me.' June held her hands up to the infinite sky. 'We haven't spoken in weeks. Am I meant to just put my life on hold while you're here?'

Edith shrugged. 'You've done that anyway.'

'I didn't want to! I was getting used to the idea of... you know. Starting over.'

Edith looked to the horizon. It seemed as if the grey clouds had poured between two black mountain ranges, rolling onto the faraway ground like a spill of white paint. 'What's that?'

'What? Oh, that's the glacier. That's where I'm taking you.'

'There!' Edith prodded the table with a heavy finger. 'That's why I'm angry! We're *going together*. Aren't we?'

June brushed a fly out of her fringe. 'That's not how it feels on my end. Might be the easiest thing for you, showing up without thinking, but to me this is...'

June chose her next word with care.

'Unsupportable.'

'June, what does that even fucking mean?'

'A few months ago I could have fit you in? Not now.'

'What do you call this?' Edith stood up and twirled with her arms outstretched. The mountains and glacier and miles of ash spun around her in a grey blur. 'You have plenty of room for me!'

'Stop it.' June snapped. 'Stop acting like a spoilt child. We're out here because...'

Edith came to a standstill and let her silence press down on June like heavy ozone.

'Because I don't know what else to do with you!'

Is that all? thought Edith. *She doesn't know where to go next?*

The possibilities were endless. They had to keep trying, keep butting up against the impossible, until it crumbled or fell over or broke or became clogged up by all their attempts to figure things out. They could be their own technicians. That was simple. You just had to thrust in your hands and fumble and something would click.

'So we keep going,' she said.

June stared at her, didn't even flinch when one of the billion ash flies landed on her cheek. 'Are you even listening to me? It's over.'

Edith tried to smile. A small adjustment. 'I meant, we keep going to the lagoon.'

'Oh, fuck off!'

June ran to the car. Edith felt the whole world shifting to best suit this effortless woman she couldn't stop crashing into, and only realised she was being ditched at the lay-by when June revved the engine. Reversing wheels spat gravel into the indifferent air.

June slid her hands under a large black stone, paused a moment to feel its smooth surface against her palms, then waddled it down to the water's edge. There, she rolled it over so that its broadest, flattest side pointed to the sky, and wiggled its point into the small pebbles underneath. She stood back and hunkered down to check it was level. A mountain, inverted.

On her monthly trips to Fjarðabyggð and back, she'd stop at the lagoon to build a cairn, adding to the hundreds that lined the shore. Some cairns were so impeccably balanced June suspected their architects had come to Jökulsárlón armed with tubes of super-glue. Her own creations never seemed to survive the month between visits.

Looking past the stone she saw the calm surface of Jökulsárlón, under which invisible currents pushed icebergs like toys. The bergs came in all shapes: some smooth and sculpted in meandering white curves, terminating in weird flourishes of gravity; others glowing an ethereal blue; still others flat, gouged and ridged, like gum peeled from a plimsoll.

She'd lied to Edith about how often she came to this quiet place, hoping it would make it feel more new, not just for Edith but for June as well. More like a holiday. A guide boat full of tourists in fluorescent orange life jackets thrummed between the ice sculptures, disturbing a family of ducks, which grumbled and splashed their way towards her. There were other birds besides ducks at the lake too: Arctic Terns, small and sharp and white, and others that looked like gulls but weren't, and would throw up on you if you got too close. Edith would have loved that.

Ditching her at the lay-by had been a good decision. *No, honestly,* she told herself, *it was the right thing to do.* The serenity of the lagoon would have been lost on both of them today. June imagined Edith throwing stones at the icebergs, chasing the ducks or singing loud to the sleek seals hiding under the waves, something juvenile like that. Hitch-hiking was also juvenile, so Edith would get back to Reykjavik just fine.

June began to build her cairn. She chose particular stones, wide and flat, and stacked them with such a focus on stability, if you didn't know it had been constructed, you'd guess they came to sit like that by accident. *This* cairn could only be toppled in an act of deliberate destruction.

It wasn't that they'd fallen out of love, not at first. The way June saw things, moving to Iceland was the consequence of an acceleration Edith had yet to recognise, let alone match. The shift had been a personal risk, but not as risky as stagnation. Expecting the trend to continue, she'd made a secret pact with herself: if after twelve months of solitude she wanted to backslide into something more comfortable—give a little patience, take some slight disappointment—then that was something she could do.

A contained experiment with obvious borders.

Trust Edith to fall out of the sky, toxic as volcanic ash, a mere month before June's pact with herself expired.

Looking up from her cairn June noticed three terns above a nearby iceberg, flapping as hard as they could to stay in place. It was an ugly berg, not too large, about the size of a minibus, shaped like a fist with a thumb sticking out. Strata of black ash marred the thumb's clear ice, frozen recordings of volcanic eruptions from a decade, a century, one thousand years ago.

A sharp pop breached the motionless air, part of a greater rupture muffled by the dark water. The thumb fell into the lagoon with a splash. The terns dove in after it, folding back their wings to pierce the lake and disappear. Two seconds passed before they shot back out into the air, one carrying a small silver fish in its beak. She wondered if the birds had somehow known the berg was about to break apart just by observing it, or listening close.

Then came a new sound, a rushing sort of rumble.

The iceberg was turning.

First it rolled towards June, dunking itself face first into the lake. Then it lurched to the left, scooping salt-water up and over itself, before flopping backwards. A tail of electric blue broke the surface, five metres long, compacted and beautiful and pure. Water streamed down its sides, giving it a shimmering, unreal effect, as if it was trying to come into being from nothing.

Not in all her lagoon visits had she seen anything like this.

The iceberg paused in its movements, thinking, feeling itself, understanding what it had revealed. Some rule of buoyancy pulled the blue ridge under again and the fist, now thumbless, punched back to sky. A scatter of ice chips and chunks plopped into the lake.

The iceberg contented itself with small turns and reveals, as if trying on a new dress in front of a mirror.

June looked for someone to share the experience. The coast was bare but for the cairns. Large waves broke upon the shore, and somewhere out there a tern had a bellyful of startled fish. For how many years had that icy ridge been submerged? For how many more would she be the sole witness, to know the shape of it?

The dirty chunk of ice that had once looked like a thumb now looked like nothing in particular. Small enough to obey unseen currents, it bobbed away from her. June followed, tracing its path along the edge of the lake. She knew where it was going.

Pulled towards the short inlet that led under a bridge to the sea, the ice would be jettisoned into the humbling expanse of the North Atlantic. There, salty waves would turn the ice around, deck it on the shore. The coast along this stretch was a photographic negative of the tropics, miles of black sand strewn with white and alien wreckage. This cast-off soot-stained nub, scarred by cataclysm, smoothed by time, would come to settle there, to melt in the midnight sun.

Feeling herself a mote of dust caught in a beam of light, June wanted nothing more than to see this piece of Iceland returned to itself, she ran along the pebbled shoreline, solid, liquid, gone.

GOLD STAR

Corned beef, spam, frankfurters, all still up for grabs: tinned towers of meat gathering dust. Casey doesn't know what to make of this. He pads to the centre aisle and does a quick scout of the supermarket. Rows and rows of barren shelves, empty packages littering the floor. He opens Dorothy on his phone. His nearest match is two miles away, but there might be technophobic grey foxes hiding in the shadows, or hopeless analogue romantics, and of course the roving gangs of lesbians, a constant worry, because they don't use the apps any more.

Casey returns to the meat aisle. He inspects the reformed shrine from all angles but can't see anything suspicious. He could fit the whole lot in his rucksack, not exactly travelling light, no hope of a clean pass through the business district, but it's worth the risk.

He gets three in the bag before pulling the pin on a rape alarm covertly taped to a tin of frankfurters.

Behind him, a freezer's frosted door slams open, followed by the squeak of trainers on tile. He bolts to the exit, jams his fingers between the broken sliding doors to prise them open. He risks a look back. Lycra calves, lightweight top, *beautiful* forearms, a fitness freak. Shit. There's no outrunning this one.

A scuffle in the street, limbs and fists and hard rubber in his face. Somehow Casey's the victor, a dented can of hot dogs in his bloody, white-knuckled grip. He packs the dogs and checks for a pulse then frisks the body. A set of keys, a sachet of energy gel and a phone with a dead battery. The energy gel tastes repulsive, but it'll keep the endorphins high en route to Janice's flat. The shoes are too small.

The rape alarm continues to howl. It wouldn't be wise to stick around. He pockets the man's phone, and checks his own. Dorothy loads. Sure enough, his nearest match is now one mile away, and closing. No pic, no chat.

As he threads his way west from the city centre, towards Glasgow's abandoned residential tenements in the west, bodies of breeders begin to show in the street, gull-pecked and grey.

Hey
> *Hey*
> *Got more pics?*
> **pic 1* *pic 2* *pic 3**
> *U?*
> **pic 1* *pic 2**

'Why are you,' says Janice over Casey's shoulder, 'looking at that?'

'Gotta get my rocks off somehow.'

'Not at the table, pervert.'

Breakfast is coffee, hotdogs and crackers an hour before noon. They split all food equally. Janice trusts Casey not to steal more than his fair share. This is her flat and he doesn't have anywhere else to crash.

> *Hiya! Good night?*
> **pic 1* *pic 2* *pic 3* *pic 4* *pic 5* *pic 6* *pic 7**
> *Yours or mine?*

'But, really.' Janice sits down. 'Why snoop through his phone?'

'Looking for proof.'

'Of what?'

'That not every man in this city is a sex-starved lunatic.'

'You still have blood under your fingernails.'

Casey hides his hands beneath the table. 'I just feel there must be somebody out there who thinks they could survive easier if they weren't...'

Janice snorts. 'Honey, I'm as good as it gets.'

He sighs, and makes wet doodles in a coffee spill. Instant, of course, the good stuff disappeared within the first few weeks of the sickness.

Is she offended? Casey looks her dead in the eye so she knows he means it when he says, 'Thank you. This works for me too.' And it's true. Sure, in any non-apocalyptic scenario, it might be unreasonable to shoehorn yourself into a friend-of-a-friend's bedsit with little to no warning, and stay there indefinitely, especially once the mutual connection popped his clogs, along with pretty much everyone else, thanks to a bizarre and swift plague. But under these specific circumstances, these specific and abominably fucked circumstances, yes, Casey would have to admit this arrangement works, and so would Janice.

'So what's the deal?' she asks. 'Trying to find romance in a dead guy's dick pics?'

'He's not dead.'

'Keep telling yourself that.'

Hey, nice smile! You look like a young Rennie Mackintosh.

Who?

Now it's Janice who sighs, and pushes cracker crumbs around a plate, and stares at the grotty ceiling. 'Casey, it's not safe. I heard there's two new folks in town trapping people and, well, you know, doing the thing. Bugchasers. Don't know how they aren't dead yet. Maybe they're immune.'

Casey doesn't know who provides Janice with information, but he knows better than to ask. They have an arrangement: he provides food, she provides sanctuary, and he asks no questions about where she goes at night.

'Sorry,' he says. 'I'm being a dick, I don't know why.'

'No, it's fine. Better to flick it than kick it, right?'

'Right.'

Hey.

Hey.

All my friends are dying.

Yup.

I don't know what to do.

Up for fun?

Casey sets the phone face down on the table.

'Giving up so easy?'

'He's not my type.'

*

On days when he doesn't have to search for supplies, Casey likes to walk around the city. There's little else to do in the flat but sleep, and he has a fear of someday finding solace in inertia, of turning into one of those half-alive people he's disturbed during residential raids, shrivelled heads cresting mounds of blankets and jumpers. Human burritos. They're not quite as far past their use-by date as all the dead people, and their eyes track you as you loot their homes for leftovers. They aren't as disturbing as the rotting cadavers of breeders, but they aren't far behind.

Casey's not proud of how he's adopted the 'breeder' terminology. He hadn't liked it or used it before the plague, back when it had a narrower definition, reducing actions of love to functions of biology. Then came the true horror of biology: a sickness that cared not for orientation, only heterosexual acts whether fresh or long forgotten, and no excess of love could change a thing. But now he needs to define himself as separate from all these corpses, and the alternative—to call himself a Gold Star, a title got for only touching *it* on the way out— seems unduly congratulatory.

So he goes for walks, just to prove to himself he's not a breeder and not a burrito, and sometimes it's inadvisable, like right now, as he races the length of Sauchiehall Street, ducking and diving between abandoned cars and busses, hiding from a man in possession of a long length of pipe and more than a few anger management issues.

From a spot in the middle of the street between two abandoned taxis, Casey catches sight of the man: sunken-faced, broad shouldered, a stocky frame turned hard by adversity, and a beard which a year ago might have hinted at leather accessories, today serving only as the mark of someone who has understandably stopped giving any fucks. Forget Kinsey, this was the new spectrum: apathetic to psychopathic. If you fell somewhere in between the two extremes, you were kidding yourself. It wasn't real. Given time, you'd choose.

The man begins breaking car windows and screaming; intimidation tactics. Casey knows Dorothy's a narc, the app feeding each of them information. Dorothy locates the man as less than 50 feet away from Casey, or Casey 50 feet away from the man. Casey could sign out and escape under a cover of non-existence—but then how would he know how close every other creep was? He'd be running blind through the city. He needs a better plan than that.

Time to catfish. He digs the runner's phone, now fully charged, from his rucksack, turns it on, loads Dorothy. An alert sounds out from the angry man's position, a creamy light yellow tone, the app's unmistakable chime. It says, *hi there, stranger, let's be friends, let's get to know each other, let's not kill each other on the first date*. The man stops smashing cars and checks his phone. It's an anonymous threesome, the runner's profile just as faceless and empty as Casey's.

A mobile in each hand, Casey makes a quick comparison—heft, durability, battery life—then throws his, overarm, down the street, where it bonks off a car bonnet. As a tactic, it's a transparent bait and switch, but he's walked into enough ambushes by now to know that it works. After what feels like an age, the man sneaks by on the other side of the taxi, tracking the stray signal. Casey holds his position until he's no longer able to smell the man's distinctive body odour.

Dorothy updates: less than 100 feet.

It's enough. He sprints up to Bath Street and ducks into the first building with an open door. A teal swoosh across the windows underlines the promise of 24 hour fitness. It's one of those gyms that used to stay open all night, unsupervised, a Mecca for protein-chugging cruisers and the occasional cabbie coming off a night shift. Casey moves quickly upstairs to where the tall windows give a clear view of the street. He avoids looking in the shards of mirror which still cling to the walls. He doesn't like how his clothes flap around his body when he moves, as if dancing to the growls coming from his stomach. Killer cheekbones for a selfie, though.

Hey.

A msg alert rings out in the still of the gym and Casey drops for cover behind a stairmaster, heart rate rapid. Did the man follow him here? He scans the cardio suite for signs of danger, but all he can see are powered-down machines and empty Lucozade bottles

Hey...

You didn't show last night.

The noise comes again—it's the runner's phone.

Me and the boys waited at The Vic for like a whole afternoon.

Fresh communication. Scrolling through previous chats Casey finds photos of what must either be two cherry midget gems sitting on a rug, or an amateurish close up of a man's torso with the flash on. Details unfold of a hookup, develop into semi-regular meets at the weekend, with not much small chat in-between, and then the plague hits, and conversation turns logistical and paranoid. Casual queries of *can u accom* and *can u travel* take on a deeper importance.

Casey considers to the new message. *Me and the boys?* The plural means the sender's one of at least three other men, making the runner one of four. In the dark of the gym Casey pops a semi. *For fuck's sake*, he thinks, but there's no denying it, he is aroused by the thought of a crew, a posse.. Four men managing not to bludgeon each other's skulls in a fight over the last existing square sausage. How did they all find each other and trust each other? It's not unfathomable, of course, that four men in the same city, none of whom had ever slept with a woman, had been friends before everything went to shit. But Casey's experience of dating was rotten with coming out stories, and mentions of teenage girlfriends. So it's unlikely. No, he decides, they must have all met *after* the plague, after the hets and bis and genderfucks had died off. You didn't get a Gold Star for nothing.

We'll be at Safehouse B tonight. Let me know you're okay.

How should he reply? What would be the best thing to say, to gloss over how he came by their contact details? *I found this phone on the*—no, no, no. Far too casual, hard to believe. *I don't know who your friend is but I'm trying to*—nope, gives the game away. Fuck it, what was wrong with *hello?* There was no need to be clever. These days simply being alive was a guarantee of personality.

Safehouse B. That could be anywhere. Hell, it could even be here, down among the Smith machines and barbells. He remembers the gym rats, how they'd share large handshakes, and stretch their backs and their necks as they swapped technique tips. Everyone walking around inside their very own suit of armour, this used to be one of the safest places in Glasgow.

Not any more. From the second floor window he sees the bearded man in the street, checking his phone and looking around for prey. *Don't look up*, Casey thinks, p*lease don't look up, please, don't look—oh, goddammit.*

Exit, pursued by a bear.

Deli husks proliferate as he nears the West End. Employing the same denial that once propelled him down this street from charity shop to charity shop, he now drops into each artisan cheesemonger, every boutique chocolatier. Ransacked for produce, their minimal chic and roughly plastered walls now appear needlessly sterile.

Ever cautious, he takes a long approach on what used to be an Iranian patisserie. The building's windows have fogged up, indistinct shapes move inside. It's a gathering. Might he have found Safehouse B by accident? Could it be this blatant? He'd expected a basement, a warehouse, not a coffee shop.

A fifteen minute wait for anything to happen. A middle aged woman, short and stealthy, turns the corner and slides up to the patisserie door. She knocks and is allowed to enter. The shapes behind the glass come together in a series of blurred hugs. Casey genuinely can't remember the last time anyone hugged him. He approaches the door, hesitates.

Another woman, older and less stealthy, dressed in grubby country gear and her long hair in a plait, opens the door wide. It's as if she's expecting friends, as if she's having a dinner party. Perhaps she is, given the number of women standing behind her. She looks him up and down, not unkindly.

'Well don't just stand without,' she says.

Voices rise in protest, the door closes, a conference commences. Casey hears snippets of old fears slowly returning.

'I thought this was a safe space.'

'Looks harmless enough.'

'No, I mean a "nice guy" nice guy.'

One outburst settles matters:

'What patriarchy, Hannah? Seriously, what patriarchy? It's gone. It's all gone! Just... just shut up, okay? Let him in.'

He counts six women in total. None of them look over fifty, and that's about all they have in common. They sit Casey down with cold instant coffee and stale bread, then proceed to ignore him.

'Where's Rosie?' says the older woman. 'She should have been here half an hour ago.'

'Southside,' says the stealthy newcomer. She sounds Polish. 'She sends her apologies for cancelling, but she's nearly finished with the school hall and wanted to get the job done before sundown.'

'It looks really nice,' says the youngest of the group, maybe a few years Casey's junior. 'I think Anne said she'd make bunting, but, you know...'

'I *don't* want to talk about Anne.'

'What about the bodies?' asks the older woman.

'What bodies?' says the woman who doesn't want to talk about Anne. 'Oh, the schoolkids? Dragged them out to the playground a few weeks back. Last I checked there were just a few left.'

'Oh, great plan, Rosie! Feed the ferals! What good's a community centre with wolves sniffing about the place?'

'Are you a lesbian gang?' says Casey.

They stop and stare at him.

'It's just, I heard there were gangs.'

The woman sitting opposite him, who is maybe called Hannah, he's not entirely sure of names yet, leans back in her chair. 'Do we,' she says, 'look like a gang?'

'And first define,' says her neighbour, also possibly called Hannah, although there may be two Hannahs, this one sporting an asymmetrical buzzcut, 'what you mean by gang.'

'We want to know,' says someone further down the table, 'which sort of gang you think we are.'

'He said already,' says one of the Hannahs. 'A *lesbian* gang.'

'Yeah, but gangs usually have...' the Polish woman searches for the right word. 'A similarity? Common visuals?'

'An aesthetic,' says Anti-Anne. 'We could get pixie cuts. Luce could let hers go long and Marie could—'

'Absolutely not,' says Marie, the older woman. 'I won't let the end of the world undo years of trying to grow it out. Anyway, for whose benefit? Amy, Lara, that lot?'

'Now, *that's* what I call a gang,' says the youngest.

'But we all know them,' says Marie. 'And they know us. It'd be pretend.'

'More attitude than image,' says the other Hannah. 'Amazonian.'

'Assholian, more like.'

'They were terrible before everything collapsed, remember?'

'They only hang out with each other because nobody else can stand their bullshit.'

And just like that, Casey's invisible again. The conversation weaves in and around past betrayals and allegiances, connections and dissolutions. All the stories have been told before to the same audience, the scant specifics included more or less as decoration, certainly not for his benefit. Loneliness knots inside his chest like a rat king.

'Shh, shh!' Polish Stealth holds up her hands to silence them. Someone's running down the street towards them. Casey pulls out his phone and opens Dorothy. Three matches, two approximately half a mile away, a third less than thirty feet. A body slams up against the patisserie corner window, hands smudging blue across the glass. Nobody inside reacts as the figure undresses, shucks their upper layers of clothing, tosses them away, their silhouette diminishing. As they kick off a shoe they lean against the window to steady themselves and leave a mess of lime green streaks. Off come the trousers, blushing fuchsia. Now naked, they bolt. As they put distance between here and wherever, Dorothy marks his two pursuers as less than half a mile away.

'Fucking art school kids,' mutters Marie.

Buzzcut Hannah rolls her eyes, 'We're not all—'

'No time to argue, pack up and get out.'

'It's just two guys,' says Casey.

'Did your app tell you that?' asks Luce, zipping up her body warmer, then her army surplus coat, then a trench coat over that.

'Is that a new coat?' asks a Hannah.

Luce does a twirl to show off the coat. 'Salvation Army. It has pockets!' She produces from said pockets a butterfly knife and some medical supplies.

Elder Marie places a hand on Casey's shoulder. 'Ditch the phone, kid. Some day those gold star geeks in wherever the fuck the internet lives will die or get bored and you'll be fucked.'

Polish Stealth opens the door and gives the street a fleeting reconnaissance. The lurid result of a paint-bomb ambush: streaks and spatters up Great Western Road, towards the city centre. A classic tracking technique of the art school clique, as effective as a sniffer dog but without the extra mouth to feed.

'They're outnumbered,' says Casey. He wants to hang around, he wants to say hello. He knows it's inadvisable but he wants to meet these men. 'We outnumber them.'

'There could be twenty of us and one of them and it still wouldn't be worth it,' says Other Hannah.

'You let me in,' says Casey.

'Marie's got a soft-spot for eggs,' says Anti-Anne.

'What's an egg?' asks Casey.

Anti-Anne does a double-take. 'Seriously?'

Marie claps her hands. 'Let's go, folks! No time!'

Dorothy reports: a quarter mile. The lesbian gang sweep out of the deli and split into pairs. Marie and Buzzcut Hannah run off towards North Kelvinside, Luce and Other Hannah in the direction of Kelvingrove. Polish Stealth and Anti-Anne hang back.

'Do you live far?' asks Polish Stealth. 'Do you need a chaperone?'

'I... no, I live five minutes away. I'll be—have you heard of Safehouse B?'

'Nope.'

'I never got your names.'

'We know.'

'Does this happen often? The meetings? How do I find—'

'It's a small city.'

'See you around.'

'Don't follow us.'

And they're gone, ducking down into the nearby silent subway. Casey hovers and hums and hahs. He should follow them. He shouldn't follow them. He should stay, he should meet the men at the end of the rainbow. He should run.

600 feet.

Polish Stealth is wrong when she says Glasgow's small. Before the plague everyone's personal maps might have been an abridged version of the city. Casey's had been a dozen bars and clubs, not many of them strictly defined as queer though they had gay nights, and a handful of cafes, a bunch of miscellaneous venues where queer things happened and familiar faces were always present. His map of the city had been the equivalent of a single street, fractured, scattered, knots of common consensus strung along a cat's cradle of acquaintances. But the real city had been unfathomable, a creature too large and too complex and too strange to comprehend by any one group of friends. Entire social networks had operated alongside each other like blind, gargantuan fish. To Casey, the people who'd managed to navigate freely between them, whether in person or digitally, by handshakes or emojis, they had been the strangest creatures of all.

And now everyone's friends were dead, every door was open.

Casey's palms sweat.

This is just like that time when a guy sent him a message on Dorothy asking if he was hung and if he wanted sucked off and sent him a video of him putting an absolutely massive glass dildo to good use and it turned out he was sort of handsome and lived in the building two doors down and it didn't matter that such behaviour to anyone not riddled with loneliness might seem borderline psychotic because Casey never did a damn thing about it and then went travelling and he didn't even get laid once in Malaysia and then when he came back his flat was up for rent and the man with the dildo had been replaced by a pleasant professional couple of breeders who went hiking on weekends and who were now undoubtedly dead same as every other cishet so who exactly the fuck was he still pretending for by being so damn respectable and exactly what would he let these men do to him?

'You're late,' Janice says through a mouthful of hotdog. She hasn't waited in preparing dinner, nor in eating his share. This has happened before. Her reasoning is if he's late home for dinner, he's dead until further notice, and won't mind if she takes advantage of this fact. He sits at the table and tries not to cry.

'I met some women today,' he says. 'They're trying to start a community in the southside.'

'Yeah? Where?'

'A school. I don't know which one.'

'Good luck to them.'

'You aren't interested?'

Janice swallows her food and burps. 'Casey, I find it hard enough living with you.'

'The feeling's mutual.'

This economy of compassion is what's kept them alive so long. They don't take undue risks for each other.

Janice rinses out the hotdog can, a hollow clattering. They hang empty cans from the windowsill to collect rainwater, and use them to pee in at night to avoid going down to the garden. They have a his-n-hers collection as a precaution, just in case, although the chances of contamination outside of sex are minimal.

'Don't get me wrong. Like you said, this arrangement works. It's probably the best combination? Well, it is for me. No drama. You know?'

'What if I asked you about where you go at night? How you seem to know everything about everyone before I do?'

'That would be a precursor to drama,' says Janice. 'You'd only make yourself more miserable, if you knew.'

'Who is he?'

'I don't want to talk about it.'

'And you lecture me about dangerous behaviour!'

'Please, Casey, don't push this. It's a thing I have, and it's mine.'

It strikes Casey, even in this horrific new world, it's still easier for the breeders. It might be their turn now to decide between celibacy or certain death, but even if they choose to live, still nobody's out to get them, they aren't dogged by old habits and fears and feuds that no longer make sense. He feels like a burlap sack of kittens being dragged to the river's edge.

'I'm going to bed.'

'It's only half eight.'

'I know.'

He slouches into the living room. A grey depression awaits him in the cushions of the sofa, worn deep and flat over the course of six grim months. He folds his skinny body into a too-tight foetal position, hugs his knees to his chest. He opens Dorothy, shielding the glow of the screen with a cupped palm.

Darren, 5 miles, last online eight months ago. SexBoi, 3 miles, last online three months ago. G, 11 miles, last online a year ago. Hung4Fuxx, 6 miles, last online two weeks ago. PowerBottomPete, 3 miles, last online one day ago. Twinkdestroyer, account suspended.

He never spoke to these men when things were good, never wanted to make first contact via this ridiculous online zoo. But it's a cruel trick, this longing, this savannah hangover. This readiness for a flash of flesh in the tall grass.

Hey.

Hey. Hey. Hey.

Hey. Hey. Hey. Hey. Hey. Hey. Hey. Hey. Hey.

His signals shoot out into the oncoming night, like flares, animalistic hooting. Let them come find me, he thinks. Perhaps they're just as hungry.

Casey, 0 miles, online now.

FINCH AND CROW DO
THE ALLEYCAT

Tiptoe on tarmac, other foot pulling pedals to starting position, Crow hunches over drop bars, waits in downpour and dark for the lights to change.

'You're doing it wrong!' shouts Remmy from behind. Crow can't see the other cyclist coming at him, stripped of all reflectors, day-glo clothing, but he's there, balanced on Great Western's dashed centre line. Suck of air, spray of road water. Remmy speeds past, headlong into traffic, and takes the lead in the Glasgow Alleycat. Crow's not about to take advice from Remmy of all people, on this night of all nights. Red, amber, green. He pushes off.

Several more racers zip past, no momentum sacrificed to the Kelvinbridge crossing. A timer clipped to Crow's radio holster beeps. He should've passed first checkpoint by now.

He needs to go faster.

But it is not so.

Held on Halloween and Valentines, the Alleycat's as close to tradition as the messenger community veers. The job attracts impatient people, transient souls, thrill-seekers, urban warriors, political radicals, shady folk who prefer cash in hand, no license plates. No such surprise most assembled choke back a cocktail of pills and booze before push off. Nobody found themselves at the starting line for this suicide mission by following the rules.

Not Crow; a long nap and a double-shot espresso was enough for him. Some of the other racers laughed when he declined a communal swig of Buckie at the starting line, but most held their tongue, because while this is

Crow's first Alleycat, he's not taking part. You're not allowed to compete if you plan the route. Even then, that's not why he's racing. Tonight, he's retracing. He's following Finch, riding his long-faded tyre-tracks.

Fastest courier in Glasgow, Finch had bragged, and had earned the title by way of a charmed negligence. Ignoring red lights, hopping kerbs, general risky conduct that secured him a regular spot in the comments and complaints pages of local newspapers. It paid to be gallus: his clients were city-wide, high profile and needy. He could've gone freelance without losing a full day's work, but stuck with the agency out of loyalty, and was rewarded with a walkie-talkie that never stopped buzzing. Go here. Go there. Go everywhere. Some days Finch would claim he was so in demand, you could put your hand on his shoulder holster feel the heat coming off his radio. Just don't give him anything fragile, not unless you wanted it delivered with enough scrapes and scars to match his face. Every day, Crow had wondered if their connection might let him sense the exact moment a speeding windscreen or unchecked wing mirror cracked open Finch's skull. There was no point telling Finch to be wary of a tragedy that, according to him, was less a matter of if, but when. The unavoidable fate of all bike couriers: to end up under the wheels of a bus or semi-trailer.

And then, last Halloween, Finch flew away.

That's the sort of loon Crow's chasing, this dank October night. Chasing, or replacing, he isn't certain. Crow knows he must follow, to rejoin the man he lost to uncalculated risk.

Crow still doubts what he saw last Halloween. Standing at the finish line at the foot of Hope Street, he'd peeked out from under Hielanman's majestic steel and glass Umbrella. The clouds were low, the rain was heavy. In the middle of the street, back and shoulders steaming sweat, his thighs pumping, there was Finch.

And then, a glimmer later, he wasn't.

It took six months of days that felt like slipped gears for Crow to accept Finch wasn't coming back.

Nor it was not so.

Ditched bikes clutter the corner of Botanic Gardens and Byres Road, their Alleycat owners fighting over a zip-lock sandwich bag tied

Finch and Crow do the Alleycat

to one of the park's fences. Inside the zip-lock there's two-dozen cards. Each one bears the image of a fool dressed in rags, clutching a rod, walking blindfolded over the edge of a cliff. The other twenty-one major arcana are strung up around the city, awaiting pickup. Crow had thought it clever how Finch always used the Rider tarot deck to mark checkpoints; Turns out it wasn't a pun. The Rider deck is the only deck that works. A full deck for every racer.

When it came to collecting the full deck, Crow had discovered the fastest courier in Glasgow outright cheated.

Finch did love a short-cut.

No, he *had loved* a short-cut.

Twelve whole months had passed and yet it was difficult to think of Finch in the past tense. He'd always seemed so present.

God forbid it should be so.

Crow doesn't stop to collect his Fool. The Alleycatters shout after him, Remmy's voice above all others: 'That's not the way to do it!'

But what does Remmy know? He's the most-kinked chain in the gang, who'd earned his nickname by hugging the sides of busses like remora to a shark. You'd be desperate to take advice from Remmy. Then again, of everyone taking part tonight, Remmy's the one who'd be willing believe Crow; that is, if Crow was interested in sharing, but this ritual was known only to Finch, and Crow planned to keep it secret. The other Alleycat contestants have no idea, no idea whatsoever, the significance of the designs their wheels now draw across the skin of the city.

Crow feels an ache apart from the ghost of fatigue.

Another red light looms at Hillhead subway; Crow obeys. The subway entrance belches out steam, and students in costume. Cody remembers Halloween parties as if they were part of another lifetime, a checkpoint in itself, one of many arranged in a never-ending loop. Just get to Christmas. Just get to Easter. Expect something to change. Hope against reason for the city council to build you an overpass out of routine. Don't look where you're going.

Crow didn't become a messenger for the adrenaline. What he wanted was to feel like he owned the city, or that it owned him. So many people took the same worn routes to the same old locations: job, gym, bar, home, bed, dream, wake, rinse and repeat. Never connecting with their environment, immediate, intermediate. Folded like origami, the entire city they knew could fit into one high rise, with the space between destinations a sort of place-holder text you weren't meant to try to read. Crow had lived that way: passed every exam, bagged every promotion, pinned pictures of friends to his cubicle wall, bought a one bedroom flat and then—felt unmoored.

There was an expectation that if he followed the signposts to the good life, if he built that nest, the sunny bird of happiness would swoop down to occupy it. But the clouds stayed low, and the rain still fell.

Crow wills the light to change, precious seconds slipping into the night.

Their receptionist quit one day. Didn't bother to show up. Crow was assigned to the front desk. In walked Finch: Lycra-sleek, sweat-fresh. A transaction, a signature, a wink goodbye, and back out into the rain. It was a chance encounter but something about it set Crow's heart ticking like a playing card clothes-pegged to the spokes of a wheel.

A diversion.

Crow bought a bike. Crow bought a helmet. Crow bought lights and Lycra and a bell. Crow signed up to a courier company, got his own walkie-talkie, gave himself over to the suck and push of transit, supply, demand. His body became functional. His sleep became smooth and dark as the freshest tarmac. His understanding of Glasgow sprawled, from rattling, ratty service bays with their rough humour, to pristine corporate high-rises, where he was greeted by mannequins in suits and pencil skirts, their tone friendly but clipped as if sensing his rejection of the corporate life. The in-betweens, the dead spaces, the doors marked for Staff Only, for Restricted Access, almost all unlocked and opened up and offered themselves to him. In kinship with the city he was second only to the bin men.

Life unfolded for Crow like a roadmap, and somewhere in the creases he'd found Finch, all thighs and knotted shoulders, a mind and heart like a fully-stocked tool kit. They met for the second time in a pub, with Remmy as their matchmaker. Crow didn't feel the impact of affection until the shock wore off, but by then it was too late. Something had snapped and mended in the time it took Crow to flip a taxi the bird.

Twice a year Finch locked himself away in a spare room to plot the Alleycat, with new routes posted to a password-protected message board. Other cities' Alleycats changed their routes each year, as a precaution against cheating, and being caught by the cops. But under Finch's direction, checkpoint changes were minimal. From year to year, the differences amounted to no more than a street or two.

'Why so cautious?' Crow asked one night, as the new routes went live. He was the first to download them, splayed out on their uncomfortable settee with his laptop balanced on his belly, after a long week of cycling against storms.

'I'm fine-tuning,' said Finch, re-hooking the Alleycat Key to the silver wallet chain he wore like it was still 1995. 'Tweaks here and there.'

'You know it's disconcerting, right? To have a secret room you always keep locked? It's proper full-fat Bluebeard energy. How's the rhyme go? Be bold, be bold, but not too bold?'

'"Lest that your heart's blood should run cold."' Finch completed the rhyme, but wagged his finger at Crow 'That's not Bluebeard. You're thinking of Mr Fox. It's a *much* older story, much more arcane. Lots of weird magic going on in Mr Fox. Bluebeard's just a cunt with a castle and abandonment issues.'

'You're avoiding the question,' said Crow.

'But it is not so,' said Finch, standing over the settee.

'Yes it is! You do this all the time.'

'Nor it was not so.' Finch relocated the laptop and crawled on top of Crow.

'Oh, I get it,' said Crow. 'It's a Mr Fox thing, isn't it?'

'God forbid it should be so,' said Finch, and slid south.

The diversion from interrogation to seduction meant Crow forgot to ask if Finch was fine-tuning something other than the Alleycat. Then he'd disappeared into a crease of the map. That's what it looked like: as if some unseen hand had crumpled him up. What had Finch done? What hadn't Crow been allowed to understand?

A series of potholes and cracks catches Crow off guard as he slips off Byres Road and onto Church Street. He brakes and swerves and stops and starts, and his nearest competitor swerves to avoid him and shouts obscenities into the night. Crow doesn't take it personally. The demolition of the Western Infirmary has left this stretch of tarmac in tatters, lorries, diggers and cranes, oh my! Would it be ironic if Crow came off his bike next to the ghost of the emergency ward, or just unfortunate?

Finch had always laughed to himself, cycling down Church Street, when he passed the small road next to the microbiology unit. Moy Street. A private joke which he never felt the need to explain, and which Crow didn't understand until after Finch vanished. He'd spent days prowling the city, hunting down reminders of the good times. He'd spent half an hour sitting looking up at the street sign before it clicked. Moy Street. Moy St. *Moist*. That's all it was, word play, but it had brought him so much joy.

Now the Western was rubble, Moy Street had evaporated, and it was too late for Crow to join in on Finch's joke, never mind mourn the loss of the punchline.

All it took to break into Finch's flat after the forensics team left was one solid kick to the door, and after three years of cycling daily, boy, could Crow kick. Looking back, he wonders if the police bothered trying to understand what they found in that room when they investigated Finch's disappearance. Hundreds of maps of Glasgow. Stuck to the walls, piled high on desks. Road maps. Aerial surveys. Hand-drawn. Google Map printouts stapled together, covering an entire wall. All dissected by red Sharpie, some cut up and re-stuck, organised by year, or by time, whatever was necessary to make sense of the collage at any given moment. An obsession with planning the race.

That is, at any rate, what the cops would see: a reckless contest for adrenaline junkies, a lunatic's hobby. If they'd even a little appreciation of the effort it took to create such a comprehensive mess, they'd have seen that here were anomalies in Finch's map-making and unmaking. One map was different from the others: the whole of Scotland, crisscrossed with ruler-straight markings, converging and splitting, like some twisted, sprung-spoked wheel, ley-lines divvying up the country along channels of ancient, unknown power.

Other documents, the older road maps, yellow and torn, had square chunks cut out of them. The absences were, well... absent. In a year of searching, Crow never found these scraps. They must have been with Finch when he vanished. To find the missing pieces, Crow had tracked down duplicates of the maps online and in junk stores. Some were rare but most were worthless, mapping a city now torn down and rebuilt, rerouted, transient. Collected and collated, the missing squares charted something stranger still.

But it is not so.

A city that never had existed.

It was a trick to calm the paranoid mapmaker: fake roads and dummy landmarks to identify copycats too diligent in their forgeries. Glasgow's grid system somewhat limited this technique, but still the mapmakers found room for odd alleys and dead-ends. For eight years Finch had led them on a hunt for these missing roads. The little shifts in Alleycat markers had been a delicate circling in, on all these null spaces, on the road to nowhere.

Crow remembers when Finnieston was nowhere, or at least next to it, notable for an ugly dockyard crane and an industrial past that had lost its way trying to catch up with the present, but now speeding down Argyle Street, flanked by gastropubs that double-up as barbershops and salons that moonlight as art galleries, it feels like Finnieston is everywhere, all at once, all the time, and it's exhausting, Crow is exhausted, he has never felt so body-tired and exhilarated and afraid all at once, and though this is a rare stretch of the race which observes the ordinary flow of traffic, he worries Remmy's right after all, that this is not the right way.

Because here's the thing about the Alleycat: it's a test of how well you know the streets—or, more often, how ready you are to attempt the alternatives. The checkpoints are proof of progress, but how you move between them is your own business. Everything is permissible, everything is allowed. Pedestrianised zones, back alleys, launching yourself the wrong way down a one-way street, of which Glasgow was lousy—anything to get to that next baggie of tarot cards. Knowing this, Crow clocked something police never could have, no matter how long they stared at these maps:

Twice a year, and twice a year only, on Valentines and Halloween, Finch took the scenic route.

Nor it was not so.

There were constants on his movements. Always cross the Clyde at Glasgow Bridge, even if taking the Squinty Bridge shaves at least three minutes off the route. Always once around George Square when he could just cut through it, dodging the hand-in-hand lovebirds or fall-over-drunk skeletons, depending on the season. Always uphill past the Necropolis where the ley-lines converged, its sentinel crypts presiding over the city. The downhill slalom on Renfrew Street, always against the flow of traffic, was the last daredevil flourish in some citywide incantation, but there was no indication, none at all, that Finch had ever known what he was invoking. Whatever door he had unlocked in the wall of the world, it had slammed shut behind him.

Now Crow understood. It wasn't destinations that had mattered to Finch. It wasn't even the journey. It was some arcane meeting point between the two: completion.

And Crow had missed him so, so much.

Coals alight in his thighs and back and shoulders, knuckles white and numb in the October rain. Lights glimmer, reflected under rubber, blurring red and green in the corners of his eyes. He doesn't stop to collect the tarot deck. Few of the checkpoints are simple: getting round the back of the Armadillo requires jumping a fence, a rickety fire escape on Lynedoch Street is hell for anyone with vertigo, and you need long arms or a litter picker to snatch the zip-lock spinning in the wet wind six feet up the side of Trongate Tower. If Crow stopped to collect each card he'd never make the final checkpoint in time, never mind the front of the pack. How had Finch done it? There was trickery afoot, that much was obvious.

This might be the scenic route but speed is still essential, small red time-trials scribbled on the maps. Some are generous, most are borderline impossible, but three quarters to the finish, here comes Finch's breakthrough: a piece of city planning so reckless it's difficult to believe anyone ever deemed it fit for purpose. A minute's zig-zagging South from Finnieston, all roads begin sloping south-east. Long ago, they pointed to Central Station, a smooth blending of the lower city centre and affluent west. But in the Sixties, the council pulled up half the city at the behest of big transit, and now these streets butt up perpendicular against the concrete cleft of the M8. A face-palm of logistics, it cuts Argyle Street in half like a clumsy butcher. Chunks of unfinished off-ramps stick into the air like shattered bones poking through the city's skin. A short-sighted nightmare with no end. How many homes, marvels Crow as he approaches, how many *lives* must have been displaced for this cold and snaking hubris? How many constant, unexamined routes must have warped and twisted in the aftermath?

Too late, the council sought to suture with a ridiculous stitch of cycle path. Too common sense to follow the natural roll of the land and reconnect the frayed ends of Argyle Street. This solution is more like a spine twisted in seizure. The green-floored strip-lit cage takes off in a dizzying spiral just before Anderston Station and bucks north over the M8, miles of traffic clotting underneath. The Waterloo Street exit doubles as an on-ramp for the motorway, floodlights spurring motorists to speed into eight lanes of road rage, and woe betide any on-coming traffic. That the City Council might try and exterminate cyclists with such a suicidal trick seemed unbelievable.

God forbid it should be so.

However inadvisable, this cycle path was a resuscitation of older, faster passage through Glasgow's open-air labyrinth. In Finch's disappearing act, it was a sleight-of-hand. Could there be other city magicians perfecting the same trick? Moving through City Halls' gold and marble chambers, rolls of Prussian blue paper tucked under their arms, swiping proposals on glassy tablets? Was someone else pitching and planning escape from the modern world? Finch didn't care. Neither does Crow. All that matters is the short-cut, that it gets him where he needs to be.

If it doesn't kill him.

The cycle path spits Crow out onto an afterthought of pavement clustered with bollards and street lights. He feints once, twice. No gaps in traffic. Bus stop. Tug on brakes, hop off pavement, double yellows. One terrifying swerve through misted headlights—

Crow's timer beeps.

Must. Go. Faster.

Something full of bullet points and definitions slips sideways off the saddle. On the long straights he peels off from the double yellows and takes his place centre-street. White dashes hiss Morse. It's a sly lean to the left, to the right, to dodge the bass-thumping plastic race-cars, the greasy white vans, the murderous taxis. Uphill. Crow catches sight of Remmy on a parallel. They match each other over the hump of Douglas Street down to Sauchiehall. Crow rejoins the race. It means nothing to him.

The Halloween crowd stumble into traffic, a jumble of foam-padded superheroes, devils in miniskirts. Remmy's ahead, barking at the jaywalkers like a dog, and who could blame him? Sauchiehall pedestrianises. Remmy peels off down Blythswood Street. Crow flies straight on. The crowd closes in. Car horns downshift to insults, thrust like sticks in his spokes. Crow wefts, Crow weaves. His tyres skid as he pulls hard across the stones to dodge a platoon of lads in army fatigues, a sprawl of drag queens, a troupe of skull-faced things on stilts. Crow's heart heaves and shunts at each turn.

Hard right. Hope Street. Home straight.

Faster.

Crow shifts up a gear. Another. Throws weight on the pedals as if jumping from foot to foot. Downhill is not enough.

Crow starts to see it: a slight delay. A white light ghosting at the edges of the buildings, car windows reflecting the headlights of some oncoming unknown. In place of his courier walkie-talkie Crow feels the tarot deck burn through his shoulder strap.

The trick is this: push off with a full deck and you never have to slow down.

Finch did love a short-cut.

The road is a mess. Gouges in the tarmac expose wires under puddles. Too fast, too fast to dodge. Yank the handles, bunny-hop. His back wheel skids on landing but something pulls it upright, slides him back to centre. Some dark hand fixes him to a path, a destination. No time to form thoughts of who might be steering.

A bus, forty-nine grumbling feet and three inches of doom, pulls out of St. Vincent Street to stretch across Hope. True to form, there's

Remmy, gliding alongside. The invisible steering lifts. Crow veers sideways, a jumped stylus. The slow-turning bus and Remmy's bearded face blur past. Remmy shouts something encouraging—'That's more like it!'—but the dark, the rain, the blaring car horns swallow him up. A vanishing point appears at the foot of Hope Street. From here, Crow should be able to see Hielanman's Umbrella but there's a fold in the world, a crease in the map. Ghost lights slip by in streaks and sparks, anchored to a horizon too close. Far too close.

It is not so, nor it was not so, and God forbid it should be so.

But that isn't reason to *stop*.

It's a special kind of risk, to belong to a life with more locked doors than open roads; riskier still to find yourself on the other side. Finch had found a short-cut and lived within it. Crow had followed without thinking, a cheat as blatant as a red light run Finch was his fateful semi-trailer, impossible to dodge, he had known falling for Finch would wreck him. Waiting for someone like that to return from the unknown was a waste of precious time.

And now the world was flickering, fluxing, flickering out.

No more faulty planning. No more pedestrian crossings. No more safety lanes. No more wrong-way one-way streets.

Unknown routes converge. Life unfolds once more, and a great nothing consumes Crow. Something close to completion.

Nowhere becomes his destination.

His handlebars vanish, then his wheels.

Then so does he.

Heavy rain falls on cracked Hope Street.

THE
COWRY HOUSE

Silt and shell swirl outside, dark brine scratching ghost fragments up against the glass. On nights like this, when I can't sleep, you could convince me the water is aware of what it's doing, that it might be scrabbling for a way in—but it is simply the sea, uncaring. Any harm it causes, the destruction its tides have already wrought, is nothing personal, nothing deliberate.

It's okay, though. Inside we're safe, we're watertight. The wooden walls creak, but they do not split; the doors rattle, but they do not burst. Occasionally after a disappointing harvest some salt-water squeezes through the letterbox but, the morning after, once the tide draws back, we skip breakfast and beachcomb all day to catch up with our transgression. As long as we appease The Hermit, we're safe from everything, forever, inside the Cowry House.

A threadbare blanket draped over her shoulders, Simone joins me by the window with a mug of steaming hot. Hot what, I've stopped asking. It warms you up when the tides are high and the air is dank. I've never learnt how to make even an unsatisfying hot, Simone's always the one to make it. This arrangement was in place long before I washed ashore.

Simone points outside to a small white dot that seems whole, not a fragment. The tips of my fingers tingle, wanting to pluck it from the black and drop it into one of the hundred sandblasted mason jars that crowd the hut's every surface.

Simone extends the blanket so it rises up her thin back, across my own, and turns me away from the window. In a few hours the tide will recede, revealing a pale sickle of beach, but before then it will drag all the flotsam and jetsam of the whole wide world over the roof of the Cowry House, down past the windows, out to sea. To watch the past's detritus drift in scraps and ribbons... it can coat your heart in salt crystals, cure you, dry you out till there's nothing of you left. Simone knows this, we all know this, but she is better than most of us at ignoring the dawn tide.

We pick our way across the lounge, dipping our feet between miniature cities of wine bottles, mason jars, scientific beakers filled with countless, countless, countless white shells. She takes me into her room and into her bed, pulls the covers over our heads. Behind hidden glass the sky's scalloped edge pushes back the sea until the Cowry House can drip onto the sand. I hear The Hermit shift in its room. It never sleeps; or if it does, the process is subliminal, a kind of rest that takes place in shifts, never quite unconscious.

The sun rises unflinching, and Daniel is first to the beach. Daniel's like a giant clam, reluctant to reveal himself soft and almost-animal. It would take more strong men than there are left alive to prise him open. He cleans the beach in the morning, removing the most horrific remnants under a sap-like dawn. If the rest of us were to see those half-buried memories sticking out of the sand we'd never set one foot outside—and then what would happen to the Cowry House? What would become of us?

While Daniel works Simone makes a pot of hot and we gather round the kitchen table. It's the only surface in the hut we haven't yet buried under glass and shell, because though the kitchen is small and rarely used to cook what carrion Daniel finds on the beach, we need some space to ourselves. The Hermit understands, I think, why we need this. Then again, it thrives in claustrophobia and sometimes I worry keeping this surface clutter-free must look like we're slacking. The guilt of laziness is a hangover from the old days, productivity a hungry deity, our personal space its ever-expanding altar.

Tilly is the last to sit at the table, long hair coiled around her head in buns and pleats. When loose, the fine blonde strands always hang as if wet, even when dry, and she can't stand her reflection in windows at night, so she grows it long, bulked by sand and salt, ties it up in ornate arrangements. Everyone else cuts their hair close. The less there is for the hermit to grab onto, the safer we are when it sinks into one of its impenetrable, violent moods.

After hot and a pan of fried periwinkles, we go outside to collect driftwood. What was once a garden drops in sanded steps to the beach. Offshore, the round Bass Rock gives a thumbs-up to the Firth of Forth, while behind the hut a cliff rises, once sharp and climbable, once tufted with wild grass, now worn smooth and slippery. Downwind, Daniel holds a ragged gull by the neck and shakes sand from its wings. This will be our evening meal. Between now and then, we search for cowry shells, ribbed and empty, small and tiny-toothed, tight white smiles without mirth. This is our payment to The Hermit, for this refuge. We don't know why it demands only cowries, the same way nobody ever figured out what use a cave of gold was to a dragon, nor power to power, which became devalued, so abundant, so hoarded. We can't ask the Hermit, can't decode the clicks and meeps which pass through its mandibles at dusk as it tallies our intake of tiny white shells. The Hermit wants what it wants, and in return we have a home.

Each day we each take one shell home to The Hermit, even if we've found more. We don't know what our host will do when the supply runs out, as it is running out already, as everything will some day run out. So we ration our salvation.

Jake is the best at finding cowries. Before they became scarce, it was as if he could wave an open palm over the drifts of sand and the shells would shiver themselves to the surface. Now, when the sea seems to have given us its all, he must place trust in his keen eye to pick out solid white curves against the infinite jigsaw of broken-down conch and shattered china. Most days he will find one cowry before the driftwood dries, and today is no exception. His daily contribution secured, he sets to work on Daniel's gull, plucking it bare, working free stubborn feather stubs with a flinty knife.

For my own part, I am not as good at the harvest as Jake, or Eleanor, but better than Simone and Tilly. Daniel is hopeless. He knows this beach better than anyone—the rock-pools that catch the most dead things, the best basalt outcrops to perch upon if you want to spear a squid and drag it, dripping ink, back to the hut for The Hermit to eat—

but Daniel doesn't have the patience needed to find cowries. When the tide turns, creeping around the base of Lionrock, crashing in firework sprays against Flatrock, or bubbling over the grey-green stones that pile in Pebble Corner, if Daniel has yet to find a single cowry Jake will step away from the camp-fire, move down to the thick drifts, and find one for him. Jake will point it out, blatant as a gold nugget, but won't touch it. Daniel must be the one to lift the shell and bring it home to sit inside a jam jar with the others of its kind. This is cheating, but what The Hermit doesn't know doesn't seem to invalidate the agreement, and we can't afford to lose Daniel. Who would act as caretaker, who of us would be able to look upon the end of the world each morning and, without complaint, get to work?

It is Tilly's job to remind Daniel of Bron, what happened to them when they got ill and refused to go collecting. I say ill, I mean depressed, but in a life carved from unhappiness, like an ornament whittled from jetsam, there's no value in the distinction. All that matters is what happened, how the wood at The Hermit's door is still stained dark with Bron's blood. We've lived with that stain for so long, it's invisible day to day, even to those of us who are skilled at looking and seeing and remembering. Those are not Daniel's skills. If anything, it's his ability to ignore what's right in front of him that makes him valuable to us. It is Tilly's job to remind Daniel. This is how we hold each other to account.

Some days when the sun is low in the sky, the sea shining like sheet metal, I'm reminded of a lover, long dead now, who said he didn't trust people who grew up by the sea. Their horizons were too far away, their skies too flat. The shore frightened him. He feared the collective denial of the beach: a pot-luck of life burrowing under, clinging onto, or teetering atop the ground-up remains of those less-fortunate. To go to the seaside is to ignore this truth with all your might, ignore how one inevitable day you will become part of the shoreline, spread as fine as dust. He was right to be afraid. Gone now is the luxury of land on which to build our wilful ignorance.

We roast Daniel's gull on a spit, but he does not join us. Eleanor, Tilly, Jake, Simone and I watch him trudging back and forth across a stretch that's more igneous rock than sand—he hopes a cowry will shine white against the black. Eleanor juts her chin at Jake and he gets to his feet, gives the fire one last rejuvenating prod before going to Daniel's aid.

While he's away Eleanor shows off her secondary haul: patterned enamel, shards of glass with their sharp edges gone, a mobile phone case with all the wiring removed. She shares her secondary haul when Jake isn't around. It's not that he isn't interested in the other items the tides return to us, but he does consider it a waste of energy—especially now cowries are becoming scarce.

Daniel and Jake return to the fire, each with a hand in their shorts pockets, clutched around a single cowry. The rest of us unthinkingly check where we've stored our own shell. When we're finished eating we throw the gull's bones to the waves to suck them clean and wash our hands in shallow pools, scattering evening sand hoppers. At first I found their translucent bodies repulsive, but have softened to them over time—in many ways we share a means of survival, and I respect that.

The Hermit is restless upon our return. The door to its room rattles as it moves around, scraping its makeshift shelter across the floorboards. It must be feeling cramped inside its unusual home—it's been many days since the sea gave us anything substantial for Simone to take apart and transform into something more spacious.

Our last gift was an oven, screws and springs rusted, presented in a tangle of green and orange fishing nets. Simone dismantled the appliance and bound it in panels to the Hermit's collaged carapace of the car doors and doll's heads, tarnished mirrors, flowerpot-halves, bound with tar and rope. The rest of us calmed the quivering naked thing in the lounge, stroking its soft, oversized abdomen. It snapped its slim claws in a half-hearted manner, compound eyes swivelling on their stalks. I don't know if it understood us, our reasons for clinging to life, our needs as human beings—if it understood how difficult it was for us to ignore our evolutionary disgust, which told us to be terrified of its twitching pleopods, pale and rootlike in the gloom. Twice it became scared and scuttled to the corner of the room, smashing bottles of cowries under its heavy, hard legs. The cabin's walls bowed inwards under the sea's pressure and we feared we'd all be crushed, swept away, dumped on some foreign shore—but we rehoused The Hermit, we survived the night, we resumed the harvest. The following day was a blessing, as was the next, and the next.

Like hoarded gold and power, however, the days devalue.

I hope for a minivan to wash up. We'd bind it to the rocks so it couldn't drift away, and we'd take off the back doors, remove the seats. The Hermit could slope out of its current patchwork house and reverse its fat bulk into the chassis. Maybe it would wheel away to the sea bed, and leave the hut to us. Perhaps its protection would wash away that same evening, that would be a blessing. None of us want to remain here until the sea rubs Bass Rock down to a salty nub.

The waves are rising now. They slap up against the windows, licking the glass to see how the hut tastes. Simone sits with me among the stacks of cowrie containers, shells packed tight and shining through the glass. She reaches for the nearest jar and removes six cowries, instructs me to sit with my legs open then mirrors me, pressing the soles of her feet against my own. We've created a small arena, and she throws the shells into it. Two land smile up, four bite into the rotting carpet. I collect them and copy her: three of each. I win. We begin again, operating under the simplest rules.

The game distracts us from what horrors sweep past the windows, tentacled and unfamiliar, or human-shaped and flaking, until that which floats has met the sun, and what will sink has sunk.

THANK YOU

Family first: Dad, for letting a very young me stay up far too late to watch The Twilight Zone; Mum, for and opening gateways to the ineffable and celestial, and our shared love of graveyards; Aidan, for all manner of adventures, cheating certain death climbing up disused overgrown quarries and down wave-battered coves. This book couldn't exist without you.

Andrew Milk, the King of Wands to my hapless Fool. ;)

Lethe Press (Steve Berman) for saying yes, and keeping the plates spinning.

Zoë Strachan, for opening the door at exactly the right time.

The good ship Gutter Magazine and all who sail in her.

The Queerdos: Sasha de Buyl-Pisco, Paul McQuade, Heather Parry and Kirsty Logan; thank you for the glitter and the grit.

And finally: Agnes, Andrew, Anna, Antje, Bart, Bonner, Brian, Bridget, Cal, Calum, Claire, Colin, Crow, Douglas, Elaine, Eothen, Fiona, Garry, Harry Josephine, Henry, Ian, Jake, Jamie, Jen, Joan, Jules, Kate, Kate, Katie, Katie, Katy, Laura, Leckie, Matt, Michael, Mulder, Rachel, Rachel, Rob, Robbie, Robin, Ross, Ruth, Scully, Sophie, Sophie, Tiu, Tawny, and countless others.

No man is an island, but we make a fine archipelago.

ABOUT THE
AUTHOR

Ryan Vance is a writer, editor and graphic designer, born in Northern Ireland, now based in Glasgow, Scotland. He created *Queer Words Project Scotland*, a mentoring scheme for emerging queer writers, and co-edited the associated collection, *We Were Always Here: a Queer Words Anthology*, published by 404 Ink.

Lightning Source UK Ltd.
Milton Keynes UK
UKHW010034280221
379494UK00001B/53